SAFE CONDUCT

Also by Elizabeth Benedict

Slow Dancing
The Beginner's Book of Dreams

SAFE

▼

CONDUCT

ELIZABETH
BENEDICT

FARRAR, STRAUS AND GIROUX • NEW YORK

Designed by Debbie Glasserman

Library of Congress Cataloging-in-Publication Data
Benedict, Elizabeth.
Safe conduct / Elizabeth Benedict. — 1st ed.
p.   cm.
I. Title.
PS3552.E5396S24 1993   813'.54—dc20   92-37077 CIP

This is for my parents, with gratitude and love

And it was in this gazing back that what is called
inspiration consisted.

—Boris Pasternak
Safe Conduct

SAFE CONDUCT

There was no one listening the first time we made love, no one keeping track of our movements the morning we met, or any of the nights we spent that first summer in Mac's apartment off Dupont Circle or my cabin a few miles north of Washington, no one watching except Otis, sixty-five pounds of shedding, effusive yellow Labrador who slept at the foot of the bed, who had belonged to Sam, and now that Sam was gone, Mac took him everywhere except to work. He could not bear to leave the dog alone.

Nights in my cabin it rained good fortune and a river of tears. We would wake after four or five hours, bleary-eyed, alert, prepared for anything. Anything but this—a feeling as powerful as a riptide. I had no idea what to do with it, it was like an extra limb, money in the bank, a feast after years of rations. For weeks I thought: It is all my imagination, I have willed myself to feel it, because this is what I want. Twice a day, I traveled from one foreign province to another: from the haunting black granite of the Vietnam Memorial Wall, where I was shooting a documentary called *Please Write*, where everyone's emotions but my own were public property, to this cabin in the woods where I shed my skin, felt it fall away and disappear for the night, a thick winter coat checked at the door.

For weeks at the beginning, we were clumsy in bed together, and weirdly hesitant. There were so many more surprising things to feel than lust. In the middle of the pitch-dark night, I would wake with a start and turn to Mac, listening for his breath. When I heard nothing, I would move closer and hold my hand against his back, firmly enough to feel a pulse, soft enough not to wake him. Then I would hold it there for a few more seconds, just to be sure, because I did not believe something so wonderful could last through the night. He was like a shooting star, a deer on the road, a firefly. You come upon them suddenly and in their very nature, they are always about to disappear. He didn't. His attention did not waver, he arrived at the cabin as eager as Otis, tail banging against the flimsy screen door as if it were a drum, as if he were leading a parade into my arms. He brought books and read me passages, he brought green cardboard containers of strawberries and blueberries and fed me berries one by one. He brought fresh pasta, hard cheese, pints of heavy cream, made us rich, sticky dinners, and let Otis lick the dishes. He told extravagant stories about the countries where he had lived, women he had known, and much quieter stories about his children.

I was used to falling for men who were bookish and quick-witted, ambitious, and excessively self-involved. But Mac had qualities I had never paid as much attention to, things you can't learn in books that I must have longed to know, about a certain kind of generosity, vulnerability, a particular species of loss. There was a directness to his feelings that startled me sometimes, or maybe what I mean is an openness to the way he expressed his grief. But when we stopped talking, we still sort of fumbled, and Mac was sweet about that too. "It's because this means so much to me. I'm not usually such an oaf."

"I'm not going anywhere. Especially with this canine asleep on top of me." I exaggerated; the dog's back, his unfamiliar animal heat, only pressed up against the soles of my feet, as sturdy as a wooden step. "I've never slept with a dog. Hardly done anything with dogs since I was a kid. Did I tell you that my first job, when I was eight, was walking a toy poodle? I wanted a better job but no one would hire me. I went all over the neighborhood. They said I had to be eighteen to work in a deli, sixteen for Woolworth's, and I don't know how old for Bloomingdale's. I couldn't wait to grow up, I hated being a kid."

"How's being a grownup?"

"Much better suddenly."

"Where ever did you come from, Kate Lurie?"

"Me? 'I come from a tough place, and I live in a tough street, and the farther you go, the tougher it gets, and I live in the very last house.' You like that?" He smiled and I felt him nod against my shoulder. "I read it in a book."

"I like this," he said, and ran his thumb across my skin.

"Which part?"

"The whole thing. The soft parts and the tough parts. I like tough women."

Tough has always been easy for me. But it was in the middle of the night, while Mac slept, that the softest parts dared to come out.

ONE

There is work you do for money and work you do for love. The films I do that matter are about people who have suffered enormous losses, their sense of smell, their freedom, their arms, legs, their children. The first time I visited the Vietnam Memorial Wall in Washington, I knew I would return to do a film about it, about the objects people left there and the lives of the people who left them. It took four years to raise the money, and the morning I met Mac, in the spring of 1988, I had been shooting for only two weeks. My cameraman and I had shown up at eight, before the crowds, to take shots of the whole of it in the morning light, and Mac was bicycling across the Mall, in runner's shorts and a T-shirt. He stopped to watch and ask what we were doing. There are always on-lookers with questions; I didn't give him a second thought. But he returned at noon on foot, wearing a dark pinstriped suit, white shirt, and striped tie, with a chicken-salad sandwich for me, two cans of Dr Pepper, and an invitation to lunch. I hesitated. In the suit he looked distinguished and very Waspy, like a judge or partner in a law firm, a Washington operator, fair and handsome in a way that had always seemed dull and a little suspect to me. I imagined he had come back to set me straight about the war or the Wall or the value of my project. But it was nothing of the kind. "I thought you might want to swap war stories," he said. "I was in Vietnam for three years."

"Fighting?"

"Just the bureaucracy. I worked in the Embassy in Saigon in the late sixties. Went back after the cease-fire for six months and then again at the very end. I helped organize the flotilla to get the Vietnamese who worked for us out of the Delta."

"I've read about that. What's your name?"

"Eli MacKenzie."

"It sounds familiar."

"People call me Mac."

"What do you do now, Mac?"

"As little as possible."

"Haven't recovered from your post-traumatic stress syndrome?"

"Hell, no. Vietnam was the most interesting job I ever had. I traveled all over the country for two solid years. The problem's been the last eight years in Reagan Country, and things took a turn for the worse last spring." I expected a revelation, a bit of gossip about the Contras or the Secretary of State or Reagan himself, but what he said was "You remember when the Circle Theatre closed? I used to go to double features there two or three times a week during lunch. Now I mostly read. I just discovered Malamud. Have you read much of him?"

"Did you have some place in mind for us to sit down with those sandwiches?" It wasn't only what he had said about Reagan and Malamud that changed my mind, it was the whole, peculiar package. I wasn't thinking romance, I just wanted to hear his take on Vietnam.

He came back every day for the next two weeks with lunch for me from the State Department cafeteria and wonderful stories about Southeast Asia, about his children, his dog, his days in the army in the fifties. He wore his government uniform, the starched shirt, the Brooks Brothers tie, but the central character in the stories was a restless idealist, a guy who really cared more about doing the right thing by the Vietnamese, by the Guatemalan peasants, the Cambodian refugees, than making his way up to the seventh floor of the State Department. A guy whose aristocratic good looks were often misinterpreted by the well-meaning wives of his colleagues, who fixed him up on dates with women from the crowd it looked like he belonged to, rich divorcées who needed escorts for Christmas parties on Embassy Row and wedding receptions at the Cosmos Club. "But these days," Mac told me, "I seem to meet a lot of twenty-three-year-olds. It's like talking to my daughter, but not as much fun."

He had come from shanty-Irish stock, had spent every nickel he'd ever made on extravagant dinners and family holidays, ski trips with his kids, the car he'd bought his daughter, Polly, when she graduated from college the month before. He looked like the men he worked with, dressed like them, could walk and talk and persuade and debate the way they did—he found his name once on a list of the brightest men in the Department—but the last eight years of Reagan had taken their toll. And Sam's death, a year before, had almost done him in.

I think now that there was nothing coincidental in our getting to know each other in the shadows of the black granite wall.

At the midpoint, where the Wall is tallest and the list of names stretches so high it feels like a wave about to break and crush you in a sea of perpetual grief, I would approach people as they left letters and gifts and ask if they would talk to me in front of the camera. It wasn't just flowers and photographs they propped against the Wall and stuck into the cracks between panels. Some days it looked as if there was a yard sale going on. There were Bibles, teddy bears, bumper stickers, Jim Morrison tapes, cigarettes, a thousand packets of Kool-Aid. There was a park bench away from the crowd where Mac and I ate lunch, and he told me his stories, and I told him mine. He was consumed with his own recent loss and I was consumed, as I always am, with everyone else's.

The cabin where we spent those early nights belonged to a friend, a place I had rented for three months to research and shoot *Please Write*. Not long after I returned to my apartment in New York, Mac and Otis followed, with Otis leading the way, straining at the leash.

A year later we were married and took a sort of honeymoon to Istanbul to see where my grandfather had been born. He used to joke that he was part Turk, though he was all Russian Jew; his parents fled a pogrom in Odessa and boarded the first ship to Palestine, which made a stopover in what was then Constantinople. My grandfather arrived the same night his parents reached Turkey. For two weeks, Mac and I were tourists in the city, but the day before we left, we wandered into a synagogue to look around. It turned out to be the Neve Shalom, and the moment I connected its name to the massacre that had taken place three years before, I knew I would make a film about the families of the slain men, and I would call it *Oasis of Peace*, the English translation of "Neve Shalom."

On our third trip to Turkey three weeks ago, to finish shooting
Oasis, Mac and Eric and I changed planes in Brussels—and
there Lida was. In Technicolor, CinemaScope, Sensurround,
a hundred times larger than life. It was a place I never imagined
I would find myself.

Here I am in another.

An editing room on West Fifteenth Street on New Year's
Eve, smoking cigarettes, which I gave up three years ago, and
looking for clues in a roll of film. There couldn't be a film
here, in these five cartons of uncut footage. There may not
even be notes for a documentary, raw material for a feature.
All I've got is evidence, and the charges cover the map. Indiscretion. Infidelity. Excesses of emotion. Showing up in
places you haven't been invited. Felonies. Misdemeanors.
Moving violations. If marriage were tried in traffic court, our
license would be in danger of being suspended. When I bought
my first movie camera at nineteen, an aging 8mm from a
pawnshop on Ninth Avenue, it was because I wanted to make
people see the world through my eyes. But I am not sure I
can trust them anymore. I flip on the Steenbeck and thread
the first roll of picture and the first roll of sound. I can operate
this machine in my sleep, thread the rolls and work the controls
as effortlessly as I tie my shoes. But tonight my fingers are stiff
and clumsy, and I have to think through every step. I have to
force myself to go through with this. Any second I should see
my image on the small screen in front of me, the face that
belongs on the other side of the camera.

There are three Steenbecks in here, two more in the room
next door, each one the size of a sprawling desk, each mounted
with a small raised screen and three pairs of plates, one pair
for viewing picture and two for sound. Some filmmakers I
work with share the space and rent out tables by the day, though

I've got this one for free tonight; someone owed me a favor. The place is empty, quiet, familiar, though I hear firecrackers in the distance, or maybe it's gunfire. In six hours it will be 1992. Midnight is my deadline. It won't take nearly that long to run through the footage but I thought I should give myself some slack, in case I need to stop and start, like someone learning to walk again. The deadline is self-imposed. Self-inflicted. Most of what I am about to watch is self-inflicted. I know it is New Year's Eve, but this can't wait until tomorrow, it can't wait until next year.

There I am, my face blurry around the edges. In a matter of seconds, I come into focus smiling and am startled by my likeness. The seasoned leather aviator jacket I wear all winter makes me look bulkier and more daring than I am, and my hair, a lighter brown than the leather, is pulled back in a low, loose ponytail that shows off my cheekbones with a boldness I didn't expect. I think of my appearance as a hit-or-miss affair, of my hair as something I need to keep away from my face, of vanity as an indulgence I don't have time for, but I wonder if I'm looking now at the woman Mac sees when he tells me I'm beautiful. Then I watch myself laugh at something he said off-screen: "Hey, Sparkle Plenty, child star of stage and screen." She was a Dick Tracy character, the daughter of a hobo called B. O. Plenty, and the diminutive "Sparks" is one of Mac's private names for me, and mine for him. Then he appears at my side, flashing a quick smile for the camera, turning his head to take in the lights of this city where we have never been. We are hauling our luggage down a narrow sidewalk from Brussels's Gare Centrale to our hotel, and my cameraman, Eric, is pretending that we're ordinary tourists, eager to record the highlights of the trip. It was supposed to be a lark, a one-night stopover with a bit of sightseeing, a few museums, and a box of Belgian chocolates for the road, a place besides Frankfurt to change planes on our return to Istanbul.

I never expected to become a subject in one of my films. They are usually people riven by loss, and my job is to record them putting their devastation into words. Sometimes, often, they surprise me—with resilience, fatalism, joy, jokes that make the crew erupt in laughter. "So I was telling my doctor what happened to me this morning. Have you heard this one? I committed a Freudian slip while I was serving my husband his coffee. What I wanted to say was 'Here's your coffee, sweetheart,' but what came out of my mouth was 'You sonofabitch, you ruined my life.' " I laugh with everyone else, but it isn't until I'm editing the films, alone, in the strained, artificial light of a windowless room, at one Steenbeck or another, that I cry. I look to my subjects for clues as to how I will endure being alone again. It could happen at any moment. This is a hard story to tell.

TWO

▼

On the screen I see a splash of brightness in the distance and the blur of a hundred anonymous Belgian profiles. The surfaces of hard things are brushed with rain, they shine like varnished wood in the glare of Brussels's lights as we trekked down the hill to our hotel making silly faces for Eric's camera. He's rarely without it, like a woman and her pocketbook, but this was the first time he'd ever turned it on me. "I'm just burning off short ends," I heard him say, because he knew I was about to ask whose film stock he was dipping into and how come. "I pulled what I had left out of the refrigerator this morning."

"Which way's our hotel?" Mac asked.

"Across the plaza to my left," Eric said. "And down five doors."

"That's not bad for a man walking backwards."

"My ex-wife said I did a lot of things backwards."

"I didn't know you'd been married," Mac said.

"Call it a youthful indiscretion. Call it the 1973 remake of *Invasion of the Body Snatchers*. After the honeymoon, my limbic functions were taken over by a pod. According to my wife."

I stop on a frame and examine Mac's face in mid-laugh, the band of his eyes and eyebrows visible between his beard and the edge of the navy-blue wool watch cap pulled down over his ears. The crow's-feet are deep, like tracks in dirt, major highways on a road map. He will always be sixteen years older than I am. But I am not looking for evidence of decline in this frame, I am looking for a sign, a marker, something to tell me who he really is, and how I could have been so mistaken. So misled. Yet this is all I detect: his lips locked in a bold smile. He's an unofficial member of the crew, and happy to be here.

We had just come upon a tiny plaza, more triangular than square, so brightly lit, so perfectly Belgian, that it might really have been a movie set, a doll's house in which you could walk around. "It was your idea to fly through here, wasn't it, Eric?" Mac said.

"Yeah."

"You don't usually have such good ideas."

"I was homesick for Stella," Eric said. "Stella Artois. And I was tired of the shakedown whenever we changed planes in Frankfurt. Taking apart the entire camera three times last trip. Besides, Kate got a deal on the tickets, didn't you?" he said to me. "We're saving sixty-two bucks."

"On each ticket," I corrected, and laughed. I'm like a miser with his money, a filmmaker with someone else's. You can't pull off a shoot like this on a budget like mine without counting every dime. We were meeting the rest of the crew in Turkey late the following night. "And Eric said he'd find us a cheap hotel."

"I've been staying at this place for years," Eric said. "Decades."

"I didn't know you'd spent so much time in Brussels," Mac said.

"Mostly changing planes on my way somewhere more exotic. And I lived here one summer in the mid-seventies, working on a film about Magritte."

The shop windows were trimmed with blinking Christmas lights and filled with gold-framed etchings, frilly lace blouses, handmade puppets, stacks of chocolate. In the windows of shops and restaurants, pastel-colored neon words hung like paper cutouts of the moon on a darkened stage. MARZIPAN. CARLSBERG. STELLA ARTOIS. FRITES. CHANGE NO COMMISSION. Two diminutive, elderly women crossed in front of us, waddled from the door of a café to a Mercedes waiting by the curb, Dame May Whitty doubles in mink coats, mink hats, each cradling a Yorkshire terrier in her arms. "Did you know you can take your dog to the opera in Brussels," Eric told us, "as long as it's wearing a suit and tie?"

"But do they let them die with dignity?" Mac asked.

"The old ladies or the dogs?" Eric said.

"It's beautiful," I said. "I don't know what Conrad was complaining about." On our flight from New York, I'd remembered that Conrad's Marlow passed through here on his way to the heart of darkness. This was where he got the assignment, where the doctor measured the dimensions of his head with calipers. Marlow said that Brussels always made him think of a whited sepulchre.

"Maybe he was complaining about King Leopold," Mac said, "buying up the entire Congo."

"Or all the goddamn dogs," Eric said, and swept the camera across the width of the plaza, Fiats and Alfas parked with one set of wheels on the curb, Baroque townhouses painted white and topped with white stone gables that belonged on wedding cakes. Sheer architectural extravagance. The camera as a languid caress over the lush surfaces.

"At the end of this street is the Grand'Place," Eric said, and pointed, "and there"—pointing in the other direction at a narrow brick building—"is our hotel. Follow me." But he sprinted ahead like a long-distance runner and left us still humping all of our luggage and his.

Mac's eyes wandered over the iridescent plaza. There were streetlights, floodlights, the fluorescent brushstrokes of single neon words in pale pinks and sky blues. The wet sidewalks and cobblestone streets were streaked with light, hurling back as much as they received. It began to rain a fine Belgian rain, soft as dusting powder. "Beautiful," Mac said, as his eyes settled on me. He meant this swatch of the city, this square: he meant me. But there was a trace of sadness around the eyes, a hint of contortion, restraint, impossible to detect unless you live with him, unless you know the key dates on the calendar of his life. There are whole seasons he cannot bear, months at a time in which he still seems to mourn. When I made the plane reservations, I had forgotten what day it was.

On the small screen in front of me, we are traipsing through the wood-framed door of the Hôtel Petite Madeleine, Mac in the lead, a tight fit with all our bags and the hand truck piled high with aluminum flight cases and cartons of film stock. He makes a big show of dropping Eric's knapsack to the floor and pretending to trip over it on his way to the front desk. I blow the camera a kiss. The clerk barely raises his head to greet us, but for a few seconds, his sallow eyes meet the camera. It's a chilly, chilling glare. We're interlopers, up to no good, and his line of work isn't tourism but embalming, interrogating, measuring the dimensions of men's heads with calipers. Or maybe this is Belgian hospitality. Then it comes to me: he is the dour, bourgeois, bowler-hatted man in Magritte's paintings, without his hat. What better place to find him than here.

"The name is MacKenzie," Mac said. "We have a reservation."

The clerk's eyes drop to the reservation sheet on the desk. He scans it, shakes his head, and declares, in almost unaccented English, "There is nothing under that name."

"Are you sure?"

"Quite."

Mac peers over the desk, obviously trying to read a list of names upside down. Then he points to one. "There, that's my wife's name."

"Lurie, Kate. A single and a double. One night?"

"Yes."

"Miss Lurie, please fill out this form." The clerk looks across at Mac, in something of an afterthought. "Mr. MacKenzie, there was a woman looking for you earlier."

Beneath the edge of his watch cap, Mac wrinkles his brow in disbelief. It can't be true, this news he's just been told.

"How long ago?"

"Oh, several hours."

"Did she—"

"She did nothing but ask. I said there was no reservation

for you. She left. We have two rooms available on the sixth floor."

The shot widens out. I'm at Mac's side, my eyes rolling toward the ceiling. It's not disbelief I see now on my face—I believe every improbable word—but irritation, on the same plane as a practical joke. I am not amused.

"What did she look like?" Mac asks.

"I don't remember." The clerk turns around to pluck a key from one of the mail slots and holds it out to me. It is my name on the reservation sheet, my name Eric must have given when he made the reservation.

"You don't remember?"

The clerk shakes his head no.

"How tall was she?"

"Complimentary breakfast is served from eight to ten in the breakfast room through that door."

"Did she have a Russian accent?"

"I have no idea."

Mac sighs and tries once more. "Is there someone to help us with our bags?"

"No."

Suddenly I'm in the center of the screen, looking straight into the camera, between Mac's face and the face of the startled clerk. My eyes are dark and direct and I see more fear in them now than I remember feeling at the time. There is no sound, but it's clear that I'm annoyed, that I'm about to issue an order. I can read my own lips. "Eric, turn that fucking thing off."

Off it goes.

There is no footage of Mac, Eric, and me going upstairs a few minutes later. There was barely room to bend our elbows in the lift. It creaked and whined, it crawled up to "6" the way second hands move on old windup clocks. Instead of one smooth sweep around the face, they sputter from second to second, sixty sputters a minute.

"So," Eric said lazily, feigning nonchalance, "who's the dame?"

"What dame?" Mac said.

If I had a clip of his face, pressed between the wall and our bags in that shower-size elevator, what would I see? A handsome fifty-year-old man in a Gore-Tex parka. Blue eyes, Celtic features, a mop of graying hair. People think he is rich, that he comes from money. They think he is a Wasp or a tweedy, somewhat disheveled professor in his worn khakis and old sweaters.

"The one who's looking for you, that dame."

"Oh, that one." Would he tell Eric who she was? "Has to be a mistake."

"A mistake?" I said. "You think the clerk hallucinated a woman coming in and asking for you?"

"He didn't seem like the hallucinating kind," Eric said.

"A woman came and asked for Mr. McIntyre or Mr. McWilliams," Mac explained. "There's no McIntyre or McWilliams. MacKenzie shows up an hour later and the clerk gets the names confused."

"Maybe in Edinburgh, sweetheart, but not Brussels."

"So who is she?" Eric asked.

"How could it have been her?" Mac said to me. "I didn't tell her where we were staying."

"Are you sure?"

"There was no reason to."

"Maybe she called our apartment today and talked to Miriam." She was my assistant and housesitter when we went away, the woman who took care of Otis. "I put this hotel on the itinerary."

"That must be it. I don't know how else—"

"You sure you didn't tell her?"

"Positive." I wanted to believe him. I'd never not believed him, but her showing up here like this—

"Is this some flame from your days in the CIA?" Eric said.

"Who told you I was CIA?"

Maybe he had arranged it all on the phone when she called yesterday and didn't tell me. But he tells me everything, in the most minute detail, a reflex to confess left over from his fearsome Catholic childhood.

"State Department, CIA, USIA," Eric said, "it's all the same cast of characters."

"Eric, do you think Kate would've married a spook?"

"Wouldn't have been my first guess. But I wouldn't have guessed a G-man either."

"She wouldn't sleep with me until I left my job," Mac kidded.

"I might have, if I'd known you didn't take the place too seriously."

"I never took it seriously," he joked. "I take it more seriously now that I'm working with all these private refugee groups. They think I'm the big expert on how to persuade the State Department to do the right thing. I couldn't figure that out for twenty-two years."

"But I thought you were in Vietnam," Eric said.

"Three times. From '68 to '70, for six months after the cease-fire, and for a few months in '75."

"Sounds serious to me," Eric said. "And possibly CIA-related."

"The second trip was. The CIA didn't have fifty Vietnamese-speaking agents to help monitor the cease-fire, so they had to borrow us from the State Department." Mac smiled slyly. "How's that for cover?"

"It has," I said, "the added advantage of being true."

"As far as you know," Mac said.

"What about Moscow," Eric said, "or was it Leningrad?"

The elevator jerked to a stop at "6." "Eric, push." He was closest to the door, and I knew what was coming next.

"They called it Leningrad when I was there," Mac said. "What about it?"

"Eric, the door won't open on its own."

"Was it serious?" Eric was staring straight into Mac's eyes, as if he were focusing a camera or aiming a pistol.

"Eric, this is not the Grand Hyatt. Push the door, unless you intend to spend the night here."

"Leningrad—" Mac's lips stretched into a smile for Eric, his eyes lit up, he was halfway to the Winter Palace, around the corner from his flat on the Kirovski Prospekt, a bottle of Georgian wine on the night table, her Levi's in a heap on the bare wood floor. "Leningrad was wonderful."

THREE

When he was still in the Foreign Service, a particularly arrogant colleague used to call him Rip Van With It, on account of the beard and mustache he has been wearing on and off for years. By their dim lights he was eccentric, outspoken, though he got high marks on what they call "interpersonal skills." A smart guy, a capable guy, but with strong opinions a little to the left. Not the best way to make it to the head of the class. He had no ambitions to become Secretary of State, or even a big-time ambassador. He just looked for jobs that would keep him engaged, entertained, and out of the country. In the spring of 1974 he snapped up the offer to leave his desk job resettling Cambodian refugees and go to Leningrad on two days' notice. Smart, capable, wildly sentimental.

I've known their story inside out since the night in his bed Mac first told it to me. It began as pillow talk and went on long past midnight, a command performance, Mac draped

across the bedsheets doing Lida's lines in Russian, followed
by almost instantaneous translations and rich, lusty laughter,
as if they were together, still laughing at all of their delicious
secrets. It was as if he were auditioning for a role in my life,
or in one of my films. People who don't know me well tend
to do that: figure I'm always working, always on the prowl for
material. But I wasn't working that night. I was spellbound, I
was all there, half in love with him, the other half with her.

It wasn't until the next morning that I saw the photograph
in a Plexiglas frame high up in the bookcase and asked if it
was his daughter, Polly. No, it was Lida. I took it down and
studied it. "So this is Lida. The face that launched a thousand
intercontinental ballistic missiles. And those must be the famous Levi's, before she took them off."

"If you like, I'll put it away."

"Don't tell me it's been here all the years since your
divorce."

"Just during dry spells. Let me put it away."

I looked her up and down. There was something long and
lavish about her, an intensity in her gaze and her smile, a ripe
curve to her hips. She was as lush as a rain forest. "So you
fucked around on your wife, MacKenzie."

"It was complicated. It was the seventies, you know, and
the sixties hadn't been easy for us. I'll put it away."

"Not until you tell me more."

For most of June in Leningrad, the city is a stage, a movie
set, a hallucination, awash in light that bears no relation to
the hour. It is not until midnight that the sun dips below the
horizon, but by one it has crept back up and turned the sky
sapphire blue. By two it is the color of robin's eggs, of Lida's
eyes. On their first night together, she left the bed and sum-

moned Mac to the window, pushed aside the drapery with the
back of her hand, and revealed the middle of the night to him,
as if it were her own creation. "I've heard about the White
Nights," he said in Russian, "I've read about them, but I had
no idea . . ." Her back was broad and sweaty against his hand,
the silhouette of her breasts in the half-light had the power of
a caress. It seemed they had known each other much longer
than this.

"Where'd you learn Russian?"

The question struck him as suspect, on the verge of their
embrace.

"University," he lied, in Russian. The only English words
she knew were a few stiff greetings and three or four obscenities.
"It's all come back in my two months here."

"You speak like a native. But you make love much better
than the natives."

She was very sly or very innocent.

On the living-room coffee table of his flat on the Kirovski
Prospekt, he kept a family photo album. He looked through
it often, pictures of his son, his daughter, his wife, and the
pair of pet turtles whose photographs the children forced on
him as he kissed them goodbye the morning he left. Most
nights he cooked a steak and read *The 900 Days*, Harrison
Salisbury's account of the Siege of Leningrad. After his first
few weeks here, the dinner invitations had dried up. The dozen
men who worked in the consulate hated the city, hated the
Sovs, dreaded going home every night to their unhappy wives.
His wife would have loathed the place too. The predictable
isolation of diplomatic life times twenty, times forty. Tailed
on every trip to the market, barely a dozen English-speaking
families in the community, none of the usual perks. No, he

didn't miss the dinners, where the only topic of conversation was how awful the place was. The lousy phone service, the stinking KGB, the rotten weather. The closest place to buy a Band-Aid was Stockmann's in Helsinki. "I haven't had a banana in two years," the wife of the CIA communicator had told him.

The night he met Lida, he closed the photo album, downed what was left of the Scotch in his glass, and headed out for dinner. It was a beautiful night, sunny and mild as a summer afternoon. He wandered up Kirovksi past the park he didn't know the name of, to the Bolshoi Prospekt, with all of its fading, melancholy splendor, its anonymous shops. You had to step inside the door and peer around another door to see what was for sale. There was hardly a street you crossed without imagining, longing for, what it had been a hundred years before. Even after two months here, Mac's heart ached at the seedy glow of the nineteenth-century mansions and the faces that entered and left them, the pallor and despair of refugees. The only place you saw them exult in public was at the ballet. They went wild at curtain calls, threw single flowers from the balconies, ran to the edge of the stage with immense bouquets.

These are the sentimental details he remembers of his time in Leningrad.

And these, much more practical: the restive crowd waiting outside RESTAURANT 25 that night. He had never been there, would not have noticed it without the crowd: there was no sign in the window or above the door. The food must have been passable, with people spilling onto the sidewalk. Next door was a blini shop, and he'd go there if there was too long a wait. Wherever he ended up, he'd set down his Russian/English–English/Russian pocket dictionary next to his plate. It never failed to start a conversation. You are English? No,

American. American! Did you hear that? He's American! Fantastic! Tell us, is it true that everyone in America has two cars? Not everyone, but some families— And is it true that everyone in America has a house? No, some people live in flats but— And what about the Rolling Stones—is it true that a black man was killed at one of their concerts in California? Even the most banal conversations engaged him. The Russians gave him the same pleasures his children had when they were very small: curiosity and innocence about all that exists beyond their borders. He pushed to the head of the line and told the maître d' he was alone.

These are not niggling details. Nor is the layout of the table where he was eventually seated: every chair but one at the end of the table-for-eight was taken. It looked like a table of foreigners, a few Arabs, an Indian, a European or two, talking and laughing in pairs or threesomes, the table littered with empty wineglasses, full ashtrays, the carcasses of chickens and fish.

He told the waiter he wanted liver and onions.

"No more."

"Then goulash."

"No more."

"Fried fish."

"No more."

"Bring me whatever you've got. And a carafe of red wine."

"English?" asked the young man sitting across from him, noticing the dictionary.

"American," Mac told him in Russian. "What about you?"

"Tbilisi. Your first time in Leningrad?"

"Yes."

"Ours too." He and his girlfriend smoked thick cigarettes and picked at the food on their plates.

The man sitting next to Mac was from Geneva and very attentive to the woman at his side. The two men at the other end, from Iraq, were graduate students. They were all jovial, all a little drunk and, from what Mac could tell, there were three separate parties who didn't know one another. He paid attention to all of this at the time and months later, when he looked back on it and reconstructed the evening for the State Department investigators.

His dinner finally came as the Swiss man at his side stood up and his date leaned over and spoke to Mac and the couple from Tbilisi in a violent whisper, in Russian. "Don't look now but there are two girls at the table behind you kissing like lovers. Really going at it! Champions!"

They turned, of course, to look.

The woman who had alerted them was Lida and the precise circumstances of how she and Mac met—their seats at the table, their first words, the intent behind them—became an issue of national security three months after Mac returned from Leningrad.

"They're taking a break now," Lida whispered. "One is lighting the other's cigarette, like Humphrey Bogart." Her date returned and Lida nudged him, but he was busy cutting up a pork chop. "Heinrich, are they so open with kisses in Geneva?"

"Who?"

"Lesbians."

"I never noticed."

"Men never notice the important things. At least they don't have to worry about getting pregnant, huh?" Lida laughed and leaned toward Mac, noticing the dictionary. "You see a lot of that in England?"

"I'm from America. You can see everything there. We're very decadent." It occurred to him to wonder whether the

KGB had every restaurant in Leningrad carpeted with beautiful women, all under orders to entice him, including the two dykes. A nice touch. But too imaginative for the KGB.

Mac spent the rest of his meal talking to the man from Tbilisi about Woodstock and the death of Jimi Hendrix, both of which Mac missed because he'd been working at the U.S. Embassy in Saigon, which he didn't bother to tell the man from Tbilisi. The waiter came by and told them the restaurant was closing, they had to get out. Mac invited all of them to his flat, including the quiet man from Switzerland and his Russian girlfriend, Lida.

"Did she seem pleased you'd invited her to your apartment?" the investigator wanted to know.

Mac started to smile as he considered the question: Lida always seemed pleased.

"Did you make a habit of this, inviting Soviets to your flat?"

"Hardly. They were the first people, the only people, who came the entire time I was in Leningrad. I was very cautious."

"Except that night."

"Even that night. Lida was with a boyfriend, Heinrich, from Geneva. He clutched her hand as they sat on my couch. I really didn't give her a second thought. We listened to music and talked about sightseeing in Leningrad."

At one point Lida stood up by the window and pointed down the street. She told Mac she lived down that way. It was a throwaway. But the next day, when he came home from work, he walked in that direction and waited for her to show up.

"You say you ran into her on the street?"

"Yes, apparently she lived nearby."

"Was she surprised to see you?"

"Very."

"Pleased?"

"Not really. She thought I was too old for her."

"Do you have any pictures of her?"

"Quite a few. Would you like me to bring them in?"

"They might be useful, yes."

That first night in his flat, he and Lida had ended up in the kitchen, refilling their drinks, and somehow the conversation turned to karate, Bruce Lee movies, some drunken silliness. Lida put down her glass and cut the air with her hands in staccato chops, pranced in bare feet like a boxer across the linoleum, and backed Mac up against his refrigerator. *Zo, you lika Rohshin girl?* The first English he had heard her speak. He was thrilled by the way she rolled her "R."

I'm afraid I do, he said in English.

Ah, you spik Eeengleesh?

A little bit, he said.

Me too. Little bit. Maybe you teach me speak it bigger.

At the door to the kitchen poor Heinrich gaped disconsolately as Lida and Mac convulsed with laughter at absolutely nothing, like people stoned on dope, when a fly on the rim of a glass of milk is the funniest thing you've ever seen.

After Lida and Heinrich left his flat that night—they were the last to go—he went after them, raced down the stairs, hovered at the second-floor landing, and watched them leave the building in the hour of darkness between midnight and one, Heinrich hanging on to her hand for dear life. Mac moved out to the front step to watch them cross Kirovski. It looked as if they were heading into the park whose name Mac never learned. He wanted to see where she lived, but they had vanished. He turned and pulled open the wood-framed door that led back inside and started for the stairs, but as he took his first step up, he turned once more and slinked back to the door, pressed his nose to the glass, but saw nothing, no one, except, across the street, four orange dots from the four lighted cigarettes of the four men in brown pants who followed him everywhere.

The night after they met, he waited at what he thought was her corner for half an hour and was about to give up when a tram rounded the corner, screeching as it slammed on its brakes. From the back door, she leaped down to the curb. Was that Lida? In pigtails, long Vermont Maid braids? Last night's Levi's, a gauzy turquoise Indian blouse—his eyes dropped. And bright red clogs. Yes, it was. She held a few record albums to her chest, and when she looked up— For a moment, Mac couldn't speak. There was a name for this, the Something Syndrome. A French writer. He is terrible with names. The Stendhal Syndrome. When you are made speechless, dizzy, by a work of art.

She stared back for a moment before she spoke. "What are you doing here?"

"I didn't recognize you in—" He didn't know the word in Russian for pigtails. "In these." He reached to touch one of them, but the second he lifted his arm, he wished he hadn't. "These," he said again in Russian, and brushed his finger against her hair. She did not take her eyes from him, did not flinch.

"*Kosichki*," she said.

"How are you?"

"Normal. And yourself?" The grammar was formal. She continued to stare as if at an elephant in the middle of the street, curious and perplexed, and held the record albums tighter to her chest.

"You told me last night about the Kazan Cathedral," he said.

"Did I?"

"You said that the nose in Gogol's story was going to end up in the Kazan Cathedral but the censors wouldn't allow it."

"I said all that?"

"And you said you would take me there."

"I don't remember. I'd—you know." She made a tippler's gesture, a fist with a thumb and pinkie up in the air, belting back a drink. "But maybe you're right. I mean, sure, why not, I'll take you there sometime. Why don't you give me a call."

"Are you free tomorrow?"

"I work tomorrow."

"What about Saturday?"

"I have plans."

"Sunday?"

"If you want to go that bad, someone from the consulate can take you. Or you can go alone. It's just down Nevsky, you know where it is, don't you?"

"That isn't really what I had in—"

"It's the building with all the columns, you know the one I mean?"

"What about a drink?"

"When?"

"Five minutes. Six minutes."

He could hear laughter rumble around in the back of her throat as if she was about to cough. "I just told my mother I was on my way home."

"I see."

"I took Heinrich to the train station."

"Heinrich? Really?"

"He's going home."

"Germany?"

"Switzerland. Geneva."

"I'd forgotten. By train?"

"Train to Helsinki, then plane."

But she still had not answered his invitation for a drink. Did she want him to ask her again? "Which building do you live in?"

She gave her thumb to the peach-colored neoclassical whose lobby he had explored earlier, going from mailbox to mailbox, as if her name, her first name, which was all he knew, might be painted on one of them next to the flat number, the numbers bold, blocklike, and runny. Some kids with a can of red paint. "I was in there before," he said.

"Doing what?"

"Looking for you."

"I didn't think last night you were so ambitious."

"I had no idea myself, but when I got home from work tonight, I kept looking out the window, looking for you, so I came downstairs to see if—"

"Well, if this drink means so terribly much to you, I suppose I—" But he could see her trying to conceal a smile as she played at relenting.

"Do you know a bar nearby?" he asked.

"No place we can sit down."

"Should we go back to the restaurant where we met last night?"

"It'll take hours to be served."

"Tell me where you'd rather go."

She seemed to move her eyes slightly to Mac's left, as if she were looking over his shoulder, and to his right, his other

shoulder. Then she chewed for a moment on the inside of
her lip. Had she seen Mac's companions? "You have a phone
in your place?"

"Of course."

"I'll call my mother from there."

They walked for some time in silence.

"Have you always lived here?"

"I was born in Warsaw."

"Warsaw?"

"My father is in the army. A general."

"Still in Warsaw?"

"Prague. They've been divorced for twenty years. I haven't
seen him in five or six years. Why do you smile?"

"Was I smiling?" He is a terrible liar. "I guess I was." Fifteen
years ago in the army, his army, he sat in a potato field on
the eastern edge of West Germany in a deuce-and-a-half with
a set of headphones on, listening to Soviet military backscatter
and translating sophisticated communications intercepts. Uncle Sam taught him to speak Russian so he could spy on Soviet
generals. And fall half in love with their daughters. Full circle.
You had to appreciate the irony, the government resources
put to such unorthodox use. "I'm just happy," he lied. "What
about you?"

"I'm normal." The word is nearly identical to the English,
pronounced "normahl." "Why are you smiling now?"

"In English, it means something else, the word 'normal.'
It's a standard against which one measures behavior, not emotion. It means"—it took him a moment to construct the Russian—"it means not aberrant."

"Oh."

"Are those new records you've got?"

"Presents from Heinrich."

She hugged them to her chest like schoolbooks and seemed not to want to talk, as if she was preoccupied or wanted him to know she wasn't really interested in him, just indulging his thirst, his infatuation. She seemed not to have remembered their vigorous flirtation from the night before. He asked no more questions as they walked through the lobby and rode up seven flights in the lift.

In Mac's foyer she tossed the records onto a chair and Mac saw the full bouquet—The Grateful Dead, Stevie Wonder, Joni Mitchell. It was not music he paid much attention to. "I'm sorry, I don't have a stereo."

"No problem, I've got a friend with one. Big place you've got. How many rooms?" Before he could answer, she had disappeared down a corridor and he could hear her opening doors, the rubber heels of her clogs squeaking against the bare wood floors. "How come I didn't see this wing last night? Maybe I did. I don't remember a lot of last night."

"Lida?"

"You sure you're here alone? What if I open this door and find your wife? She's come for a little visit. Oh, hello, Mrs.—" She called to him down the hall. "What is your surname, please?"

"MacKenzie. Look, Lida—" There was something he had to tell her, something he should have said before.

"This is a very good room. Good view, good bed frame. But why aren't there any pillows? Not a sheet or a blanket? Whose place is this? Did you know I'm married too?"

Was she kidding or just trying to even the score? But that could wait. Where the hell had she gone? He peered around the edge of a door expecting to see her.

"This must not be your bedroom," she said from somewhere

else. "No sheets or blankets on the bed. Where's your bedroom?"

He found her across the hall. "Next door. There's something
I need to—"

"You should have brought your family with all these rooms.
You sure you're not a big shot in the Party or maybe the
Komitet?" Soviet slang, her slang, for the KGB. "You have
two children or three?"

"Two."

"Maybe when you leave—just between us—my mother and
I can take one of the rooms. But I think we would prefer—"
She wandered back across the hall to the first room. "It needs
curtains and a rug and a bedspread, and of course some pictures. Whose furniture is it?"

"It belongs to the consulate."

"I thought maybe you swiped it from Lenin's Memorial
Flat. Have you been there? If you haven't, skip it. I'll take you
to the Kazan, but forget Lenin's place."

He cut in front of her and grabbed her wrist, harder than
he meant to.

"What the hell are you doing?"

"Listen," he whispered, "this place is bugged. My car is
bugged. I'm followed everywhere. I should have told you
before."

"Is that all?"

Mac nodded.

"I'll be all right, I've got plenty of friends."

"Are you sure?"

"Of course."

"I just wanted to—"

"What happened to the drink you promised me? Have you

got a Heineken?" Then she was off again down the hall, opening doors, passing judgment on the wainscoting.

"How do you know about Heineken?"

"Everyone knows. It's the best American beer. Why do you laugh? What is this, a room for a dwarf?"

"It's a walk-in closet. Look, why don't we—" He was trying to herd her down the hall toward the living room. "You said you were married."

"To a Jew. This room is much too small for my mother and me. A friend of mine from Siberia." For a moment Mac thought it was a joke. "He was in my class two years ago at university, and when he graduated, he didn't want to go back to Siberia, so I said, Look, I'll marry you, that way you can stay here. It happens all the time, it's called a 'fictive.' We got married, but you know what happened after that?"

"What?"

"He wanted to fuck me! Can you imagine? I think *this* is the best room so far. It even has a toilet. Now he's trying to get out, to go to Israel. Wants me to come with him. If I did, his family would put us in the same room and he'd get ideas. I can't speak a word of Jewish, I wouldn't be able to explain. That's all I need . . ." She was talking nonstop now, like a parody of Soviet manners: on the street and in the lift, they spew surly monosyllables, but behind closed doors, you can't shut them up. "Don't get me wrong"—she turned and looked at Mac—"he's a nice guy. And I have nothing against Jews. I would even marry one—I'd marry another one—if I loved him—" She had managed to lead them to the arched entranceway to the living room, where she stopped and hooked her thumbs through the belt loops of her Levi's. "What a mess we made here last night." She laughed. "I'm surprised you invited me back."

Mac was a little surprised himself. "I'll be right in with the beer."

"The room looks much bigger with no one in it. I see you bought some souvenirs. This is very good for a little girl, a Matryoshka doll. How many dolls are inside her? You have a daughter, right? This must be your wife. A knockout. Excellent teeth."

What had she found in there?

"This little girl, is this yours? What's her name?"

The photo album on the end table.

"Polly."

"I like Polly already. And the boy?"

"Sam."

"I like Sam too. The wife, what's her name?"

"Babette."

"And who's this?"

"Here's your beer. Don't you want the glass?"

She shook her head and kicked off her clogs, drew her legs up onto the couch and crossed them Indian-style, maneuvering the album onto her lap. "Who's this?"

"A friend of Babette's. That's the beach in Dominica."

"That's in America?" She took a long drink, tonguing the mouth of the bottle.

"No. The Caribbean. Near Haiti."

"Where's this?"

"It's a hotel in the States where they have ducks in the lobby. There are my kids—they're looking at the ducks from that couch."

"Why are there ducks in the lobby?"

"During the day they're in the lobby but at night they take the elevator upstairs to the roof to be fed."

"Someone carries them?"

"No, they just waddle onto the elevator. Of course the elevator man helps them."

Lida looked up at him with a grave expression. "This is everywhere in America?"

"No, just this one hotel called the Peabody. In Memphis. That's in the state of Tennessee."

"Of course. Elvis Presley. Blue suede shoes. That must be you. Without the beard and mustache." She squinted as she looked at him, sitting now across the room. "I prefer the face with the hair. You look like Tsar Nicholas. Why are you looking at me that way?"

"What way?" Was his hunger as obvious as her pigtails?

"Don't get ideas about me. You're much too old. I didn't think men so old even want to do it anymore."

"I'm only thirty-six."

"A relic." She laughed. "You also look like what's his name, that singer, Kris Kristofferson." She sucked on the beer bottle and lowered her eyes to the photo album. How old was she? She had mentioned university two years ago. Twenty-three? "I like these pictures very much. An American family. And what does this do?" She gripped the beer bottle between her knees and held aloft the album, pointing to a photograph on the bottom right.

"It cooks food. Mostly meat."

"An oven?" She returned the album to her lap and drank again.

"It's for cooking outside, it's called a—"

"And who's this woman at the oven?"

"She was our maid when we lived in Haiti."

"How many maids do you have?"

"None now. We don't have them in the States, only when we live abroad."

"Why not?"

"It's too expensive in the States."

"I see."

He was relieved that she kept her head down so that he could stare at her undetected. She studied the photographs like an anthropologist or an art historian. Or a spy. Could they have gotten to her so soon, just since last night? Anything was possible. But the quality of her interest in the pictures was genuine. Or was it? She turned the plastic-covered pages, smiled at certain pictures as if she had her own memories of them. Very sly or very innocent. He would keep watching, he would have to keep his eye on her. If he detected a hint of duplicity, self-consciousness, a case of nerves, he would walk away. He could do that, luscious as she was, and lonely as he was, he would walk away if he had to. But for now, he stared, gaped like Humbert Humbert longing for Lolita across her mother's living room. Though there was nothing pubescent about Lida. Lo-Lida. Well, maybe the pigtails and the rock 'n' roll. She looked up suddenly. "What happened to the radio we were listening to last night?"

"It's in the kitchen. I'll get it."

"I'd love another beer. Why are the children in costumes?"

When he returned to the living room he explained Halloween and squatted to plug in the radio.

"Is that a KLH?"

"How do you know about KLH?"

"That's the kind my friend has."

"This is a Grundig. It's German." Mac was on his knees, pushing the settee to one side in a search for the outlet, trying so hard not to overwhelm her with his desire that he felt he had retreated into a kind of obedient dullness. "How did your friend get a KLH?"

"His father's Commander of the Leningrad Military District. He's got his own flat, his own car, his own everything."

Mac steadied himself against the wall, his back to her, the plug in his hand. Was this bait? Had he been mistaken about her? Had she choreographed this so smoothly that she had fooled him up to now? He inserted the plug and turned to her. A beautiful woman in pigtails smiling at pictures of his children dressed up as Peter Pan and Wendy. If they had gotten to her since last night, she would not be tipping her hand like this, letting on that her friend was the son of the most powerful man in Leningrad. No, if she was working for them now, she would keep that bit of information to herself. If she turned— he would cut her off immediately. But in the meantime . . .

"That's great," she said.

"What is?" His foolishness, his gullibility?

"That's Janis Joplin. 'Take Another Little Piece of My Heart.' Make it louder. Dance with me. But don't get any ideas." He opened his arms and started toward her, keeping time to the music. "No, no, no, not like that. Like this." She gyrated toward him and then slithered back, swinging her hips, snapping her fingers. She moved like Janis Joplin but looked like Judy Garland in *The Wizard of Oz* with the pigtails, the huge smile, the schoolgirl's rounded cheeks. She closed her eyes and drew her arms around her shoulders, slow dancing with herself. A foot from Mac's face, she languidly opened them again, as if from a deep sleep. "Have you been following me?"

"I confess."

"What did you do with my beer?"

"Right here." He held a bottle in each hand. "Yours and mine."

"How long did you wait for me on the street?" She pulled

hard on the bottle and slinked back to the couch. An invitation to follow? He sat down a few feet from her.

"Half an hour."

"What if I hadn't shown up?"

"I don't know. I would have come back."

"And if I'd shown up with Heinrich?"

"I'd have invited you both to dinner."

"Poor Heinrich won't get to Helsinki until tomorrow morning."

"That's too bad."

"I forgot to call my mother. Where's the phone?"

"In my bedroom."

"You lure me into your apartment to make a phone call and the phone just happens to be in your bedroom?"

"I'll sit out here on my hands while you call."

"How do I know I can trust you?"

"You don't."

They were standing face to face in the long, darkened corridor she had explored before, and he touched her cheek with his palm, felt her lean into the warm cushion of it.

"What did your mother say?"

"I should marry him."

"Who?"

"Heinrich."

Mac lowered his hand, curled the fingers into a fist.

"He proposed to me tonight. At the train station. We would live in Geneva."

"Oh." It took Mac a moment to find his voice, this man whose job it often was to keep the conversation going in any number of exotic languages. "That's wonderful. Congratulations."

"My mother thinks he has good manners. Which is more than I can say for you."

He took her hand and walked her back to the living room. "And what do *you* think about Heinrich?"

She sat down on the couch, took a long swig of beer, seemed really to consider the question. "He does have good manners." She looked up at Mac. "Yes, you can sit down next to me. I won't bite you." He was not afraid of her, only of how much he wanted her. Their elbows touched. He was nervous, almost breathless, like a teenager. He had been alone for two months in Leningrad, and for more months than he cared to count in Washington, living with Babette, sleeping in the same bed, but not sharing much more than their devotion to the children. When he got home, they would try again; they had been trying again for years. But this time he would plan a trip for them, a splendid holiday. "I don't love him," Lida said.

"Who?" He had lost the thread of their conversation.

"Heinrich."

"But you'll be out. Then you can do whatever you want. You can get a divorce and—"

"Be all alone in a strange country?"

"You'll make friends. It's not so difficult, someone like you."

"Maybe if I were a man. An American. Then you do whatever you want, right? I saw a movie, *Easy Rider*, the whole thing is motorcycles and fucking. And marijuana. Here we have only fucking and marijuana. The police have motorcycles. I told you about my friend with his own flat. Well, last year on Lenin's birthday we had a big party there, music and drinking and lots of noise. The neighbors called the police. A dozen motorcycles showed up. They made more noise with the motorcycles than we made with The Grateful Dead. They banged on the door! Open up! Open up! We wave them in.

Come in, come in, we are celebrating the birth of Lenin!
Greetings to the leader of the working class! Never mind he's
dead as a doornail. We push beer and wine on them. But
we're on the job, they say. Aw, come on, have a beer, join
the fun. Well, maybe just one. When did you ever hear of a
Russian who turns down a drink? So much for the neighbors'
complaints. Next thing you know they're complaining about
the police!"

Lida, Lo-Lida. She did not look like a girl or move like a
girl, but the stories she told—they sounded like high school
but with a twist, and it was the twist that thrilled him: she
refused to submit to the vast, crushing will of the place, not
in the principled way of dissidents, but with a plucky insou-
ciance he knew was available only to the elite. She had friends
with foreign stereos, friends who would protect her from the
KGB, the way rich Americans have stockbrokers, bankers, and
family lawyers, a battery of men to protect their fortunes and
their family name. He reached into her lap for her hand. "I
like your eyes," he said. "I can't stop looking at your eyes."

"To tell you the truth, my eyes are very popular."

"I'm not surprised. I'm sure all of you is very popular."

"Shhhh. Listen."

"To what?"

"This song." But it was not one that Mac knew. "What does
it mean when he sings"—here she spoke English—"keep on
truckin'?"

"I think it means to keep on, to continue."

"Continue what?"

He wasn't sure. He hadn't lived in the States for most of
the last fifteen years. His slang was outdated, the rock 'n' roll
songs he knew were as old as Lida. "Maybellene, why can't

you be true?" Now *there* was a song. "Continue living," he
said in Russian. It was not much of a translation.

" 'Keep on truckin,' " she repeated. "That's good."

"This is good too," he said, and raised her hand to his lips.

"It's forbidden," she whispered in Russian. The word is
nelzya. He kissed her palm and she murmured, "*Nelzya*, Mac,
nelzya."

"Wake up," she whispered, and reached for his hand. "Come
look."

She led him to his window, the city from seven floors above
the street, pushed aside the drapery with the back of her hand,
and watched him gasp at the color of the sky. "But when I
drifted off, it was dark out."

"During the White Nights, it's only dark for an hour. In
half an hour the bridges go up. Have you seen them? From
here we'll see the Kirov Bridge. It looks like a giant insect with
broken wings."

The skyline was spare, even, dotted with gleaming gold
spires. Dostoevsky called this the premeditated city, laid out
according to the violent will of Peter the Great, who forced
tens of thousands of his people to live here, to build the city
on stone and wooden piles along the swampy islets and to
inhabit it all the days of their lives, the serfs and noblemen
both. Mac had read somewhere that Peter had hired the great
architects of Italy and made them prisoners too. But what a
city they had dreamed, what a sky they had to work with. Gold
domes, gold spires fine as needles, against this backdrop of
iridescent blue.

"I haven't stayed up that late. The Americans I know here,
they all have families, little kids. I got dinner invitations during

my first few weeks, but they dried up. No great loss. I have a friend, Susan, an American girl who's a nanny, I've taken her to the Kirov a few times. Otherwise, I've been something of a—" But he didn't know the word in Russian— "A man who—a religious man who lives with other men. Not a priest."

"A homosexual?" she said, laughing.

"A monk," he said in English. Then, in Russian, "A man who has no sex. Who is not allowed."

"Poor darling."

"I'm sorry I left you alone." There were words here and there that he tripped over, that he didn't know, but by now the language came to him as easily as his own history. Sometimes he dreamed in Russian, sometimes he dreamed that he and his boy, Sam, were playing baseball in the living room of his flat, and Sam shouted to him in Russian, "You're out, three strikes you're out," and Mac knew Sam was talking about their family and Mac's place in it. "I don't usually fall asleep like that, afterwards . . ."

"Nothing between you and the nanny?"

He shook his head and kissed her shoulder. Her curiosity surprised and aroused him, the hint of jealousy, possession, proprietary desire. With Babette—they were practically roommates. What time did you get in? Late. Did you have a good time? Good enough, she would say.

"What about you and Heinrich?" Mac asked. He didn't really care, but she seemed to like this game so much, and maybe Mac liked it more than he cared to admit.

"He wanted to," Lida said.

"I'm sure he did."

"But I said I wasn't ready. You know, you were making strange noises while you slept. Were you dreaming?"

"I must have been. I still am."

They swayed across the floor to the bed, they had known each other for two days, or was it only one? They had met last night in the restaurant, and then he had paced the street where she had said she lived, and then she had come up here with him. That was only a few hours ago.

"What would your wife think about you in bed with a Russian girl?"

"I'll find out."

"How?"

"I'll tell her about you when I get home."

"You're joking."

"Not everything. I'll tell her your name, but I won't tell her what beautiful eyes you have and I won't tell her—"

"You're not joking."

"She tells me who she sleeps with."

"But why?"

They lay facing each other, fists against cheeks, elbows to the mattress, a swatch of damp sheet between them, and his wilting erection, and now his wife. "It's difficult to explain." And he had never been asked to put it into words. Lida waited as if he had not finished his sentence, as if he was about to deliver the punchline to a very clever joke. Eyebrows raised in anticipation, she was an avid student now of American manners and marriages. She must have thought him capable of wisdom or wit, this girl who had been riveted by snapshots of his family barbecue. "We're going through a rough time."

"Oh."

"And we don't want to get divorced." He had nothing wise or clever to say about any of it.

"Oh." Her tone was puzzled but still patient: any moment now, he would reveal how it was that a wife did not mind her husband in bed with another woman, because even women who had their own lovers did not cut their husbands any slack.

"We decided to give each other more freedom, to loosen the bonds a little."

"Is this normal in America?"

"These days it is, more and more."

"It's like here. People get divorced and live in the same flat, you know, and have lovers, because there's nowhere else to live."

"That's not exactly—" But maybe it was close enough. "It's something like that, except that we're not going to get divorced." Did he really believe that he and Babette were going to pull through? Or was it just his last best hope, something outrageous to wish for when you blow out your birthday candles? He couldn't admit to Lida, much less to himself, that his marriage was coming apart. Or maybe it hadn't quite yet. Maybe that happened once he got home. "Let's look at the sky again. Come stand with me."

"I'll wait here and watch you."

He pushed aside the drapery, touched his thighs to the windowsill while the rest of the city slept. Lida was behind him, and the sky, this extraordinary night sky, was all he could see. He remembered the sky at dawn along the Grand Canyon as a boy, skies as clear as glass, halcyon days. He was all innocence and wonder, like Lida examining snapshots of his American family: the world now had another dimension. "You know, all my images of Leningrad come from black-and-white newsreels when I was a kid," he told her. "The Siege in the dead of winter when the trams didn't run and they pulled bodies down the streets on sleds. On my plane from Washington I was reading a book about the Siege. All the photographs were black-and-white, Lake Ladoga frozen solid, the convoy of trucks moving across it, transporting food. So when I arrived—it was early April—I half expected it to be winter, and I had no idea the city would be so colorful." His eyes were steady on the golden needle of the Peter and Paul Fortress against the pink-tinted clouds; he had read that during the war a mountaineer scaled the gold tower and camouflaged it with gray paint. "And no idea it would be so sad." Was she listening? Had she fallen asleep? Would she rather he did not remind her?

Nothing had prepared him for this, not living in Kuala Lumpur or Saigon or Port-au-Prince. There, you knew what to expect and you were not disappointed. Tropical poverty, war, flamboyant desperation. But here—he had expected to confront the second great superpower, the enemy he had been taught all his life to fear and despise. He had always resisted the rhetoric, but had at least expected, when he arrived, to understand what had inspired it in others. Instead, he had found a city of magnificent boulevards, a hundred canals, sumptuous palaces painted turquoise, bright yellow, fuchsia, paint flaking off in pieces the size of playing cards. Façades done up like fancy coffins, columns, pilasters, caryatids. Mac thought sometimes that if it were not for the muscle-bound caryatids holding up the buildings, the city would collapse. It might yet. Everyone dressed in their hand-me-downs that didn't fit and didn't match, refugees in their own land. By the churchyard around the corner, Mac had seen old women lined up to sell their belongings, a dishtowel, a pair of rotting shoes, two forks. He had been instructed all his life to fear Russia, but the morning of his arrival, he knew there was never a chance he would. The driver who met him up at the airport pointed out the obelisk in the middle of the street as they headed for the city. "We are two miles from the center of Leningrad," the man explained with funereal solemnity. "The obelisk marks the front line and the gate to the city. The Germans never made it beyond the gate." How could you fear a whole country of people in mourning? Even the children seemed to be grieving. Even the children were our enemies.

He turned and saw Lida stretched languidly across the bed, hands clasped above her head, one leg bent at the knee and splayed against the sheet. Her eyes were closed, her smile faint and mysterious. She was the only decoration in his bedroom, the only personal touch. Nothing had prepared him for her either. A voluptuary in the city of mourning.

"Are you sleeping?" he said.

"I'm wide awake."

She was ripe, she was extravagant. He stood at the foot of the bed and stroked her ankle, the furry hair along her shin. "What time do you have to be at work?" he asked.

"Nine."

"I'll give you a ride."

"I should leave here at six. I don't want my mother to know I've been out all night. I told her I was at my friend's flat. The guy with the KLH."

"Tell me about the Siege."

"The Siege? I was born in '51."

"But didn't you—"

"You want to know about the Siege, we'll go to Piskarev."

"What's that?"

"I'll take you sometime."

"Did you have family who died?"

"Of course." In Russian "of course" just means yes; it lacks the abruptness, the impatient edge it has in English.

"Who?"

"My father's first wife. My mother's first husband. Their children, their brothers and sisters. After the first winter, after her children died, my mother was evacuated to Tashkent, like Anna Akhmatova. My father was at the front. They met a few years later. They were forty when I was born."

"Any brothers and sisters?"

"She had two miscarriages before me. Then they called it quits. Then they got tired of each other." She motioned with her forefinger, more in the mood for love than history. "You sure there was nothing between you and the nanny?"

"The nanny?" He had almost forgotten she existed. "I don't need a nanny. I'm much too old."

"And no one else? Haven't you been lonely?"

"Can't you tell?" He was sure there was nothing more obvious than his loneliness, except this fistful of skin taking shape again between them.

"And your wife—are you sure she'll be happy you're in bed with me?"

"Lida, I don't want you to think that this might turn into something else, I—"

"Come on, I'm kidding. Don't be so serious all the time."

"But I am serious." He did not mean to sound stern. He ran his hand down the length of her voluptuous torso. "Serious about this."

"You are, aren't you." It was not a question. She stretched her back against the bed. "Very serious."

"And this."

She nodded, made a faint sound that came from the back

of her throat. Her back arced, her legs fell open. When he looked up at her face, eyes shut, cheek hard against the pillow, he noticed a small scar. For a few seconds it distracted him. Then her hips began to rock, and he was surprised to hear her speak. "Let's give them something to remember."

"Who?"

"The Komitet. And everyone else who's listening."

FOUR

Here is another place I never imagined I would find myself: on the verge of phoning B. J. Rose in London, on New Year's Eve. I've been tempted to call him since I got back from Turkey five days ago, five days early, but I don't know whether I want advice from him or solace or just to say I'd been thinking of the way we used to smoke cigarettes together, the only people either of us knew who still did, two junkies with a foul habit in some hotel room or other, and that I had begun again. One question would lead to another and he would coax it out of me, the whole story, draw me back into his orbit and make me long for the tortured simplicity of those days. Sometimes he would wear his wedding band and sometimes he would leave it on the night table next to whatever bed we'd slept in, and I remember staring at it, a plain gold circle, as if it were the lock of Muhammad's hair they display in the Topkapi Palace—utterly ordinary matter that to those who believe is sacred. I wasn't staring because I myself believed, but because

I could not imagine the lives of those who did. B.J. believed, in his way. He knew what it meant to take it off at night and put it on again in the morning. He was mine and then he wasn't. He loves me, he loves me not.

In the dark of a midtown hotel room one night, he did a dance step with his hand on my back. "This is how they speak to each other when they make love," he said. He meant the deaf. He had just finished shooting a documentary for the network, where we had met years before, on the debate between teaching deaf kids American Sign Language and teaching them to read lips. Then he did that same little dance step in the small of my back one more time. "I just said, 'I love you.' "

"Oh."

"Twice."

"Is it easier to say in sign than in English?"

"I love you." He was quiet for a moment. He had never said it before. Neither had I. "No. Easier in English." Then he grazed my back with his fingertips.

"How would you translate that?"

"You have a wonderful back."

"Say it again."

"Listen, Kate, maybe someday we'll get married. What do you think of that?"

I turned away from him, his feather-light touch, the place on his chest I lay my head. "The odds are better that we'll both go deaf." I spoke plain English. "Shit, I'm out of cigarettes."

"If we get married, we'll have to stop smoking."

"The deli on the corner is open all night."

"Maybe we could live in Mexico. I'd like that. On the beach. In Zihuatenejo. You could always wear your bikini. Or you could just roll around in the wet sand like what's-her-name in *From Here to Eternity.*"

"If you had just said 'I love you' and left it at that—when you said that on my back—that was wonderful. But then you went off about our getting married and ruined it."

"Ruined it?"

"You think I'm here because I expect us to get married? I'm not dim. This ridiculous daydream of yours—" I reached for one of his cigarettes and let it dangle between my lips, felt around the night table for my lighter, the one he had given me. "And mine."

"Maybe someday—"

"Forget it."

"Say you marry someone else—"

"If I get married, it will be to someone else."

"Will you still sleep with me if you do?"

"Jesus, I hope not."

"Why not?" He sounded so wounded.

"I'm not going to have that kind of marriage."

"What kind?"

"Like yours."

"What's wrong with mine?"

"Ask your wife." I heard in my voice the ready cynicism of people resigned to small portions. I was not much over thirty and already bitter as bark. "Next time you see me, I won't smoke," I told him. I sounded like a magician promising a fabulous trick: Next time you see me, I will disappear. Next time you see me, I will decide that I want more than this. "I hate it, despise it. I dream once a week that I'm dying."

"I dream that every night."

"Really?"

"Yeah."

"You have to stop, B.J."

"So do you."

"Do you see my lighter?"

The only present he ever gave me was that lighter. Gold-plated, Dunhill, it must have cost a hundred dollars, but I don't think he bought it for me. I think he bought a new one for himself and gave me the old one, passed it off as fresh. "I've got something for you." He handed me a velveteen box that looked as if it held a necklace. But surely he had not mistaken me for a woman fond of jewelry. It was much too heavy besides. Inside was the lighter, it doubled as a paper-weight. If it were new, it would have come wrapped in plastic or paper, something official and unblemished. But I took it from him, I went along with the ruse, as I went along with all his secondhand endearments, the longing I was never sure was genuine. Or this: it was genuine but intermittent. Like a latent illness. You can only be sure you have it when it flares up.

I stopped smoking two years later when I moved to Washington to research and shoot *Please Write* and live for three months in my friend's vacant cabin north of the city. It was the carriage house to a mansion that sat high on the banks of the Potomac. Just a few miles from the White House, the river is wild, the terrain is country, it could be West Virginia. I woke one morning with a nicotine hangover, deep rings under my eyes, the aftereffects of a night of cigarettes and dreams of dying, and walked down the wooded hill to the river. The path was well worn, well tended, part of a National Park; there were trees and wildflowers, a hundred live things I couldn't name. I know roses and carnations and mums, flowers you pick from the florist's refrigerator. "The country" was what we called anyplace not Manhattan when I was a child. That morning in the country north of Washington—it was early, spring, the sky was lavender and filled with birds. All I knew was that they were not pigeons. I wasn't going for distance, I just wanted to make a splash big enough so that I would remember it. I walked to the edge of the water and hurled the lighter, like a good-luck coin, into the river. I did not want to die anymore, even once a week in my dreams. Two weeks later, when he was on his bicycle on his way to work, I met Mac.

And two weeks after that, he spent his first night in the cabin. Some nights there, his tears ran down my bare arms and over my shoulders like warm rain, and he would whisper something about Sam which I usually could not make out through the tears and then could not bear to ask him to repeat. But during most of our nights there were stories to tell, the grammar and history of our lives to reconstruct, while Otis lay at our feet on the bed, the first dog of my life.

"I was like Otis for the first ten years I spent in the State Department," Mac told me one night.

"You slept twenty hours a day?"

"I was naïve. I just tried to find jobs that weren't boring, and I figured everyone else's intentions were as honorable as my own, so I ended up in Haiti, El Salvador, Malaysia, Saigon. I didn't play the game. I didn't know there *was* a game for years. My father was a printer, my mother was a seamstress. I was the first person in the family who went to college, the first one who finished high school. By the time I picked up on the game and had some sense of how to play it—by that time I knew the rewards weren't things that mattered to me. I wanted to help curb the death squads in Salvador, but I didn't care to become ambassador to Burundi. As naïve as Otis but not nearly as happy."

"But you didn't do so badly, did you? You were the some-thing or other in El Salvador."

"The consul general. It's not exactly ambassador to Moscow. You know, a few years ago I saw my personnel file. In the early eighties, someone put my name forward to be consul general in Moscow. Then they looked through the rest of the file and that was the end of that. Part of my agreement after the investigation was that I couldn't work in the Eastern bloc again. They thought I wouldn't be able to control myself. I wouldn't have, if you'd shown up. When I first saw you at the Wall that morning, I thought you were handsome and a bit stern. All business. I almost didn't come back. But when I did, I saw the other side to you. It was like Dorothy Malone in *The Big Sleep*, when she unpins her hair and Bogart almost gasps at how voluptuous she is."

"But I didn't do anything to my hair, it's always pulled back this way."

"It had nothing to do with your hair. It was when you finally decided to have lunch with me. The quality of your attention changed. It was very sexy, very intense. You were all there. I still can't believe that you're listening to me and not judging. All the women in my life have sat in judgment on me. My mother, my older sisters, my ex-wife. I figure it's because you make the kind of films you do, that you can sit and listen for hours."

"There are plenty of men I wouldn't listen to for five min-utes, and I think I've slept with all of them."

Mac laughed. "You know, this is the seashore, right here."

"What is?"

"In *Never on Sunday* Melina Mercouri plays a jovial whore who can't stand the endings to all the Greek tragedies. She rewrites them so that everyone goes to the seashore. 'Then

Medea and Jason and their children got in a chariot and they
all went to the seashore!' That's what I want for all the people
I love, to go to the seashore. I thought if I wanted it badly
enough, my wife and kids and I would make it . . . But this
is my happy ending, right here."

There was in the quality of his grief, in his own surrender to
it, an allure I did not admit to him, that I felt embarrassed even
admitting to myself. I lay awake one night in his arms thinking
of the wounded men in my life, and the name Oceanside
Gardens came back to me, as if it were a movie I had seen a
dozen times, instead of the name of the garden apartment
complex on Long Island where we lived when I was young.

In the living room of our small apartment, my mother sits
in a straight-backed chair at a card table, coloring a stack of
black-and-white photographs for fifty cents a picture, and
watching *The Twilight Zone*. It is 1960 or '61. I'm in a diminutive kid's wooden rocker, in my parents' room, watching
the same TV down the hall, on the sly. I am five, maybe six.
My younger brother and sister are asleep in our bedroom, and
my father is still in the city, at Sardi's or the Oak Room or
"21," with his friends Sam and Coco Tucker, who call my
mother "the warden." I don't know what this word means but
when my parents fight, on weekends, that is what he calls her
too. "In the immortal words of Coco Tucker," he begins with
a flourish, like a prosecutor in his closing argument to the
jury, as if he is fighting for someone's life, perhaps his own.
The Long Island Rail Road schedule is etched in his long-
term memory like his Social Security number, but the time
of the next train doesn't ever surface without prompting. Some
nights my mother calls him at the Oak Room or "21" to remind
him. Some nights she calls him at the Tuckers' apartment on
Park Avenue and Coco hands him the phone: "The warden's

on the prowl again." And some nights my mother just waits, at the card table, with fifty family portraits mailed from a photo lab in Far Rockaway. Each comes with instructions for how to color them, like painting by number. "Mother: brown hair, blue eyes, beige dress. Father: black hair, brown eyes, gray suit. Girl right: blue eyes. Girl left: brown eyes." She works with tubes of oil paint and toothpicks and bits of cotton that she twists around the tips of the toothpicks and uses instead of a paintbrush. Soon the job will be obsolete, but for now there must be something soothing about the simplicity of the instructions, the promise that family life can offer all these innocent smiles, these perfect moments, when there is so much evidence to the contrary.

It must have been on *The Twilight Zone* that I found the first man whose sorrow broke my heart. It is an episode I watch on the sly one night with my mother down the hall in the living room, though I don't remember the poor man's name. He has just been fired from his job and starts hanging around a bar. Before long, someone gives him a gift, a stopwatch with extraordinary properties. When you press one of its buttons, the world comes to a dead standstill, everything and everyone but the man in possession of the watch. Off he goes, my man, to the local bank with a shopping cart. On his way through the front door, he presses the magic button and sure enough —it works like a charm. He sails through the bank and into the walk-in vault pleased as punch, passing bank clerks frozen now like George Segal sculptures. What a clever fellow. What a lucky break. He fills up his cart with cash, zips through the lobby and out the front door—and the watch drops. The face cracks. No problem. But when he presses the button to make the world go again, nothing happens. Nothing. Everyone is

as still as stone, about to take a step, finish a sentence, go on
with the rest of their lives. He looks up, hopeful for another
few seconds that the watch's powers are limited to land. But
planes are suspended in midair like Christmas decorations on
the ceiling of a department store. His cart of money is worth
nothing. I am five or six, freshly bathed, in pajamas and bare
feet, rocking alone in my parents' bedroom, my heart aching
for this stranger. He is stunned by what's happened. One
minute he's poor, the next he's rich. And now he will be alone
forever.

My mother and I sat that way for a year or two of nights, she
painting gray eyes green, and me in her bedroom, watching
over her shoulder, watching *The Twilight Zone, The Million-
aire, Alfred Hitchcock Presents,* shows in which fantastic things
happen to ordinary people. A man knocks on the door bearing
a check for a million dollars, no questions asked. The world
comes to a grinding halt, kiss it goodbye. In real life, my
mother's job as the warden became obsolete, like her job coloring black-and-white photos: they decided that we would
move from Oceanside Gardens, where our neighbors sold
shoes and drove Pepperidge Farm delivery trucks, to Manhattan, where my father came home after work and sat in the
living room with a pitcher of martinis and a pair of binoculars,
studying the windows of Walter Cronkite's building four
blocks away, looking for disrobing women, looking for evidence of Walter, whom my father described as our next-door
neighbor to casual acquaintances. I don't think we ever
brushed elbows with him on Third Avenue, but the city was
full of celebrities close enough to touch. One afternoon President Kennedy rode in a motorcade down Second Avenue,

right past our building, and another day, Jayne Mansfield ate a tuna salad sandwich with a pickle on the side in our deli down the street.

When my father put down the binoculars and picked up his drink, he used to hold forth on the subject of his day at work, as part owner of a new company that manufactured women's bathing suits. My mother would listen and nod, and I suppose she was grateful that he came home every night and did his drinking in the bosom of his family, where it was cheaper than the Plaza and he could run a tab at the local liquor store. Our dinners began with his fabulous promises— new toys, a trip to Disneyland, an apartment in Uncle Walter's building—and ended in blizzards of accusation, the decibels mounting like bad debts. I was the only one who kept quiet, and it was barely noticed when I got up and went to the room I shared with my sister now and sat out the meal on the floor of our closet, listening for silence beneath the hems of our petticoats.

On Tuesday nights, my mother made us take a taxi to a room downtown painted dull green, a place she said was for Jewish people with problems and not a lot of money. In the waiting room were plastic dump trucks, wooden blocks, stacks of *Life*. A woman with a bun and a plaid skirt would come into the room and tell my mother it was time, and my mother would turn to me and ask if I wanted to join them tonight. "I have no problems," I said every week. "I'll wait out here." And away they would march to a small room at the end of a hall, while I sat between the dump trucks devouring *Life*. There had been a devastating earthquake in Alaska that had lasted for twelve seconds. The photograph was of the earth split open like a log axed almost in two, and I think it was in this way I learned that terrible things can happen in the time it takes to snap your fingers. I was only nine but I knew that my childhood had been over for years.

B.J. was shocked when I told him. "To the diplomat?" he said.

"Former diplomat. Unlikely diplomat."

Long silence on his end of the phone. He was calling from London, where he has lived since I've known him.

"He's moving to New York," I said.

"Oh." Another pause. "Do you think it would be all right if I called you now and then?"

"Not in the middle of the night."

"I haven't done that in a while."

"It's been a while."

"Well." You would think I had told him I was dying, he was that discomfited. "Congratulations."

"I thought you'd never get around to it."

"It's just that I'm surprised. I didn't think you were the type. You were always so—" He stopped abruptly, catching himself at the truth.

"What?"

"Lonely."

"I always thought that was one of my virtues," I said. I could hear him muffle a laugh. "I didn't need much taking care of, but I was grateful for what I got. Like a plant that doesn't need a lot of water."

"I'm going to miss you, Kate."

"You haven't seen me in more than a year."

"I'm going to miss you anyway."

"Same here."

"I suppose this means you'll have babies."

"I'll have a stepdaughter, a big one. Twenty-two."

"And no babies?"

"We might have dogs. I wouldn't mind three or four."

"I had no idea—" But then he caught himself again. No point pressing the matter, not at this late date. That clinched our separation even more finally than news of my upcoming marriage: I had become a dog lover, vulnerable to the charms of small creatures who needed me. B.J. knew and I knew that meant I would be that much more impervious to his own reckless charms.

I don't believe in happy birthdays or happy families, don't believe that any of us will make it to the seashore, but when Mac told me that he did, in the cabin, I was enchanted: I was tired of men who were as frightened and cynical as I was. All the way to the seashore, can you imagine? We're lucky to make it to the corner in one piece. There is a chance my husband won't live through the night, a possibility that when I call out his name down the hall, he won't answer. When he is fifteen minutes late coming home, I imagine not a traffic jam, a stalled subway, gridlock, a whim, but a call from the police. I check the hour again, to see who might be home, just in case I need someone to come with me to identify the body. Now and then people ask if I have children, and then, if I want them, and all I say is no. But the truth is that I could not bear to love anyone else as much as Mac, and with children, they say, you love them twice as much.

The rest of my family—we are scattered across the country like billiard balls, every one of us fallen into a separate pocket. The one I miss most of all is my grandfather, whose childhood memories of Constantinople I went in search of two years ago with Mac, just after he died. He was easy for me to love, a man of few words and gentle bearing, not much given to reflection and tight-lipped about his losses. There was nothing frayed or fraught in our history, nothing difficult in our present. What I regret is that I never found a way to talk to him about his dying, the way he languished in the bed of a nursing home for a year after his stroke, learning to write again—TUESDAY, JUNE, SUNNY SKYS—and slowly losing his mind. He died sitting up in a wheelchair, after dinner, and the phone call came two weeks before Mac and I got married. I spoke at the funeral, but never saw the body. Have never seen a body. All my experience of death is from a great distance. Sometimes I think that my experience of life is from the same distance, and that this must be my preference. It cannot be a coincidence that I married a man who had already had and lost a family. He brings proof of my worst fears but spares me the anguish of living through them myself. Every year on Mac's birthday, I do the usual corny things, the cake, the presents, and the song, but I lie about his age. To myself and whoever asks.

He wasn't fifty three weeks ago in Brussels. He hasn't been fifty for years.

FIVE

Our room at the Petite Madeleine in Brussels was like a ship's cabin, as small and plain as it could be. You opened the door and looked down at the bed. Even that—wide enough for two but shortened, clipped at the foot, like a cigar. It made me think of Jean Seberg's room in *Breathless*, the little cubicle where she and Belmondo made love and walked across the bed because it was the easiest way from one side of the room to the other, and it made me think of all the sad hotel rooms women in Jean Rhys's novels check into, hole up in with their bottles of wine and their heartache. I pushed aside one panel of the flimsy lace curtain, aware of Mac behind me, fussing with a suitcase. Outside was a narrow ribbon of city street, a lighted tower in the dark sky, and the distinctly chipper honk of a European police siren, a sound so jaunty, so linked in my mind to the sound track of certain foreign films, that I hardly connect it with trouble nearby.

"I'm going to call Lida," Mac said.

"Where?"

"At her house outside Paris."

"If that was her downstairs, she won't be home."

"Her husband might be."

I had assumed it had been Lida in the lobby—she must have called our house and gotten the hotel name from my assistant—but Mac's insistence that it wasn't had lulled me into thinking he would drop the subject for the next three weeks. But roping in her husband now—I hadn't begun to consider where he fit on this map.

"I can't seem to get through," Mac said. "I'm dialing the numbers it says to"—there was a typewritten instruction sheet taped to the wall—"but all I hear is an echo."

"Call the front desk."

"Now there's no sound at all."

"Keep trying, sweetheart," I said as though I meant it.

He sat at the head of the bed with the phone, and I sat at the foot, flipping through Frommer's *Belgium*. Lousy phone service might keep us occupied for the rest of the night, but tomorrow we could do the city in peace, until our flight to Turkey at seven. And then we'd have three weeks to prepare for our meeting with Lida in Paris. In the meantime—the Museum of Ancient Art would open in the morning at ten. Or would it? I read the details again. Admission is free. The hours are 10 to 1, and 2 to 5. It is closed Christmas Day and every Monday. I turned to the next museum and all the others in the list, watching as their doors slammed shut one by one in my face. "Mac."

"What."

"The museums are closed tomorrow."

"Could you please tell me the country code for France? You said before it was thirty-three, but every time I call that number, I hear a—I'll try again."

"I can't believe it. Every museum in Brussels is closed tomorrow. How can they do this to us?"

"Just a second, Kate."

I turned to the section on Bruges. *A city arrested in time. A Pompeii or a Brigadoon. An urban portrait caught as if by stop-frame photography, of a community that died while it still was young* . . . It was only an hour away by train, and the museums were closed on Tuesdays. "Mac, let's do Bruges. We can spend the day there and be back in time for our flight. Or we can go to Waterloo. It's only ten miles from here. Did you know that?"

"Hold on." He was dialing, listening, cursing. Then he'd hang up and start over. When he told me she had called our apartment yesterday morning, I had just come in from a last-minute meeting with Isak Kazes, a Turkish antiques dealer on upper Fifth Avenue who had heard about *Oasis of Peace* from a friend whose cousin had died in the massacre. I had unlocked the front door and caught Mac three feet from me, grinning, reaching for the knob. He had heard me coming. I grinned back. I had something to smile about. "He's going to kick in eight thousand. Not bad for a morning's work. I brought us some lunch from the new deli down the street."

"You'll never guess who called."

"Isak? Did he change his mind? Does he want to give me more? Come in the kitchen. I'm starved. All I had was coffee before I went to see him." I had draped my coat over a kitchen chair, taken foil containers from the paper bag, and begun undoing their cardboard covers. "What have we got to drink?"

"It wasn't Isak Kazes who called. It was Lida."

I was not certain I had heard right, and I turned and stared at him. Was he about to elaborate or admit he was kidding? He smiled and nodded and tilted his head toward me, as if to coax some of the glee he felt out of me, as if I wasn't picking up on my cue. "The face that launched a thousand ICBMs?"

He bobbed his head, still beaming. "I can't believe it."

"Neither can I." I turned back to the table and my eyes fell on the aluminum pie tins of jambalaya and corn fritters. I had just lost my appetite. "So how's the phone service between here and Leningrad? I mean, St. Petersburg. I guess the KGB isn't around anymore to breathe on the line."

"She called from Paris."

I started to press the cardboard covers back on the food again. It was something to do with my hands, something to fill the void where my appetite had been. "How nice for her. First trip?"

"She lives there. In a suburb."

"Too bad, I mean that she's stuck in the suburbs." Then I began to remove the covers I had just put back on. "You want the corn fritter on the same plate or on the side?"

"You're not worried, are you?"

"Should I be?"

"Of course not. She's married. To a Frenchman."

"So was Emma Bovary. Have a seat."

"And she has a child."

"Good. She's probably put on a few pounds. Could you pass me a napkin."

"Remember Susan, the nanny in Leningrad? She's getting married next week in Chicago. Lida's going to her wedding. She'll be in the States for the first time."

"Rotten luck, huh? Our being in Turkey for three weeks."

"I told her that. Then I remembered we had this stopover

in Brussels. I invited her to visit us there on our way home. She said, 'No, no, you come to Paris.' It's only a few hours by fast train. She said something about meeting us at the train station and going for lunch. At least I think that's what she said, between her English and my rusty Russian . . . I said I'd talk to you and call her back."

"How did she find you?"

"I was so stunned to hear her voice, I forgot to ask. Listen, Sparks, you've got nothing to worry about."

"I want it in writing."

"If she wanted something from me, I'd have heard from her long before now. Let me call her back and tell her we'll meet her in Paris."

"Both of us?"

"Don't you want to meet her?"

I don't know why he imagined I would. It's true that I had always felt toward her like an astronomer with a favorite star, admiring a spark of brilliance out there in the Milky Way, a few hundred thousand light-years away. But I never dreamed she would fall to earth and land on my doorstep. That wasn't part of our deal, Lida's and mine. I looked up at Mac. He was smiling, animated, waiting impatiently for my reply. "Let me give her a call before it gets too late."

I must have nodded and mumbled, "Okay." I must have been reassured by his reasoning and comforted by the likelihood that marriage and motherhood and the bourgeois pleasures of Paris had tamed her, that age had taken its toll. "Tell her we'll be there," I said. Then I tried to put her out of my mind, to move her, like a stage prop, a piece of furniture, into the background of a quaint Parisian street scene for the next three weeks while I finished shooting *Oasis of Peace*. And I

was doing a pretty good job of it, until I learned she had beat
us to Brussels barely twenty-four hours later.

Mac got a line to France. "*Allô, Philippe?* . . . *Je m'appelle
Eli MacKenzie, je suis un ami de Lida. Oui, Mac du Washington . . . en anglais? . . . bien* . . . Fine, thank you. Yourself?
. . . Good . . . As a matter of fact, I'm in Brussels, yes,
Brussels, and I was wondering whether . . . Really?" Mac's
face brightened. Mine dimmed. "What a terrific surprise . . .
Do you have the name of the hotel? . . . Yes, I have a pen-
cil . . ." He wrote and nodded and read back what he had
written. "Thank you, thank you very much." He hung up,
rattled off the news—"That was her husband, she's at a hotel
here with some friends"—and reached again for the receiver.
    "Small world, isn't it?"
    "May I speak to one of your guests, Lida"—he consulted a
piece of paper for her married name—"Martelle. Thank you."
He half-covered the receiver with his hand and spoke to me
sotto voce. "He knew who it was instantly. He said he'd call
her to the phone. She's at the bar."
    "Terrific."
    "Once you meet her, she's hard to—" Then he spoke into
the mouthpiece. "Lida! You're here! What a wonderful surprise. We came to our hotel just a few minutes ago and the
clerk said a woman—" He turned over a book of matches on
the nightstand. "The Petite Madeleine . . . You're kidding
. . . Twenty? . . . Yes, we'd love to, that sounds great . . .
My wife and I and our friend Eric . . . Let me write it down,
just a minute . . . Hôtel Saint-Simon . . . Okay, I'll ask here
at my hotel . . . We'll get a cab and be there soon . . .
Dosvedanya." He dropped the receiver in its cradle and leaped

up. She was close enough to touch, around the corner, across town, and all you had to do was hail a cab. She had even left her husband home. Good going, Lida. "This is fantastic. Did you hear all that? I guess you did."

"Uh-huh."

"She's with friends at the bar of her hotel. They drove up from Paris and we're invited for a drink. She's friends with the guy who owns the hotel. He's Russian. And that *was* her downstairs."

Mac turned to the dresser on which he'd laid his suitcase, unzipped it, and started to hum. "Let's see. I know I packed my navy turtleneck. Or maybe I didn't. You know"—this was louder—"she went around to twenty hotels looking for me today. Ours was the last one she hit. Isn't that something?"

"Twenty hotels?"

"That's what she said."

"Mac, what's wrong with this picture?"

He turned to look at me, as if I were the image out of focus. "I don't know, what's wrong with it?"

"For starters, she's three weeks early. And she's in the wrong country."

"She saved us a trip to Paris."

"Don't you think it's peculiar she spent so much energy looking for you? Doesn't it—"

"What's so peculiar? She didn't know where we were staying."

"Why didn't she call our house and get the name of the hotel from Miriam?"

"Maybe she figured we'd already left. Why would she assume there was someone in our house with an itinerary?"

"None of this strikes you as anything out of the ordinary?"

"Kate, sweetheart, yesterday you wanted to meet her in Paris."

He pulled a fresh turtleneck over his head and for a few moments his face disappeared. Then there was a loud knock at our door, and tucking the shirt into his pants, he stepped forward to open it. "Eric, come on in. If you can find room."

Eric stepped over the threshold, hands in his leather aviator's jacket, and looked at me sitting cross-legged at the head of the bed. I think it was permission to enter he was looking for. He might have been listening at the door, or he might just have felt the tension in the air, the molecules bouncing. It's what makes him a good cameraman, a devilish curiosity, a nose for danger, an instinct to stick around when any fool can see he ought to leave. "Spartan quarters this trip. They gave me a cot to sleep on, and I've got to disrobe in first position. Decide where you want to do dinner tonight? We're a few blocks from the Ilot Sacré and a few hundred restaurants. What's Mr. Frommer got to say about them?" He also has a gift for small talk that puts nervous people at their ease, though it's usually the people we're filming who need the tranquilizer most.

"The clerk was not hallucinating," I said. "We're going to the bar in Lida's hotel for a drink."

"So she has a name. A good Slavic name. Lida. I think it means beloved of the people."

"She certainly seems to be," I said.

"How'd she track down our hotel?"

"Perseverance."

"Come with us," Mac said. Did he want an ally or just someone to keep me company while he and Lida reminisced?

"And bring your camera," I said. "We'll get some stock footage."

"Of what," Eric said dryly. "Hotel bars in Belgium?"

"You can't be serious," Mac said to me.

I wasn't, I just wanted to see if he would squirm. "I want a shot of your face when you lay eyes on her. Especially if she looks like Mrs. Khrushchev."

"She won't appreciate it," Mac said.

"I thought she loved getting her picture taken."

"What time do you want to get going?" Eric asked.

"As soon as I brush my teeth," Mac said, but made no move toward the bathroom. "Really, Kate, I don't think it's polite to show up with a movie camera."

"Eric, why don't you get the camera and meet us in the lobby. Load the mags with two rolls of high speed. There may not be much light in the bar."

"What'll you want me to shoot?" he said.

Mac turned and huffed three steps into the bathroom with his Dopp Kit, closing the door behind him.

"What's the story with her?" Eric asked.

"Very photogenic. Or she was last time he saw her. He took stacks of pictures."

"When was that?"

"Seventeen years ago." I had opened one of my flight cases and was looking for the cassette player. "Is it still raining out?"

"It always rains in Brussels."

The bathroom opened and Mac said, "I just remembered the pictures. Can I put them in your shoulder bag?"

"What pictures?" Had he brought pictures of her?

"The photographs of Polly and Sam I brought to show Lida."

"Yeah." Now I remembered. "Sure. Give them here." While we packed last night, he decided to bring them, pictures of his kids to show her. "Eric," I said, "we'll see you in the lobby."

"You didn't tell me what you want me to shoot."

"You'll figure it out." I don't often have to tell him where to point the camera, and he doesn't always listen when I do, but his instincts have never been wrong. He shut the door behind him while I looked through another flight case for the cassette player I always take for emergencies. It's modified for crystal sync, and the sound is only fair, but our Nagra was with the sound recordist we were meeting the following night in Turkey. The cassette player fits nicely into my shoulder bag. I dropped it in along with two sixty-minute tapes.

"I need some mad money," I said to Mac, though I was surprised it had come out that way. All I had meant to say was "money."

"What?"

"I didn't change any money at the airport, I thought I'd do it later tonight." He reached into his pocket for his bill clip, not meeting my eye. "Not that I think you'd do any of the things my mother always told me I'd need mad money for. Fink out on me. Get drunk. Run off with another girl." I smiled and waited for him to look at me. He didn't. "Thanks, Sparks," I said, and took the crisp bills from him.

"What the hell's going on? Are you making another movie?"

I didn't know exactly what I was doing, but I knew I needed all of my armor. I knew I was scared. *You have to be mad to use Soviet rubbers. I think they're made of cardboard. We improvised. Like crazy. What we'd do is we'd—* I was heading into occupied territory, even if Mac had an idea we were on our way to bingo in the church basement. I looked at his face, the crow's-feet that fanned out around his eyes and the beard

that was mostly gray now, and wondered if Lida would recognize him, if she would be surprised, as I often am, at how
old he is. I remembered the Delmore Schwartz story in which
a young man imagines sitting in a movie theater watching a
movie of his parents' courtship. When the father proposes, the
son leaps up and shouts, "Don't do it! Nothing good will come
of it!" As we prepared to leave our room I felt a little like that
son, about to see my husband as a virile younger man fall into
the arms of an insatiable Ninotchka, and I wanted to plead,
"For God's sake, don't."

"This is what I do when I don't know what else to do," I
told him. "I shoot film. I stick microphones in people's faces.
If it makes Lida uncomfortable, I'll stop."

He mumbled, "All right," and led the way out the door. I
had hoped that my candor, the softening of my position, would
soften Mac's too. But he just waited nervously for the elevator,
staring up at the needle above the door, watching it move at
a snail's pace from "1" to "2." He could barely stand still. I
opened my bag to double-check on the cassette player and the
tapes. All there. Had I told Eric to bring fast film in case the
bar was dark? I'd ask again when we got downstairs. The camera
has always been my shield, my safe conduct through war zones,
the bulletproof glass partition between me and the hazards of
real life. But Mac travels lighter; Mac believes in happy endings, and he hates to quarrel. I think he went along with my
wanting to get this on film because he would rather keep the
peace than win the point. He's inclined to say yes to everyone
who matters to him, certain that this time, maybe this time,
all the people he loves will make it to the seashore.

"Let's take the stairs," he said, and headed toward the landing, wired with enthusiasm, the way he is when he rolls around
on the living-room floor with the dog and howls to him in

their private language, the way he is when he goes to the airport to pick up Polly after a long absence, or meets me at Penn Station when I come in from a trip, aglow with love and corny affection in the Amtrak waiting room, and a handful of flowers, as if we are college sweethearts with a weekend in the big city to look forward to.

SIX

———▼———

I have my hand on the speed control of the Steenbeck but it isn't moving. I am looking at the frozen image of myself on the screen, my mouth still locked open at the "o" in off. Yesterday at home I went through Mac's cartons of mementos for the old photographs of her. The most sentimental man I have ever known. In one carton are photographs of his parents, his children when they were small, letters from his high-school girlfriend, notes she scribbled on the corners of lined sheets of paper and passed down a row of their English class to him in 1955. "Unforgettable," says one, in a girl's neat script. "That's the song I used to sing to her," he told me. "She made fun of my voice, I can't imagine why." In his file cabinet across the room is a file on me in the top drawer, an active file, every dumb note I've ever left for him, ticket stubs, even boarding passes, the receipt from the florist where he bought me the bouquet of flowers I carried when we got married. We got dressed in a hurry, took the subway downtown to City Hall by ourselves, and went out after for Chinese. It hadn't occurred to me to carry anything, until Mac brought home this bouquet. The only feminine frippery I indulged in. Our only bow to tradition, except for the slice of cheesecake from Cake Masters we fed each other on the IRT going home, laughing until tears came.

The official Lida file is also in his file cabinet, in the bottom drawer. An inactive file. There are typed letters and onionskin copies of letters, any number of opinions on the subject of his conduct and her intentions. Something she wanted very badly from Mac that didn't show up in those documents, typed on State Department letterhead, was jitterbug lessons. She also wanted him to write down the words, in English, of the song they heard Sarah Vaughan sing one night on Radio Luxembourg while they slow-danced in his living room. *You do something to me, something that simply mystifies me. Tell me, why should it be, you have the power to hypnotize me.* She smells of wine and sex, cigarettes and musk oil. He sings along in her ear, but after four or five lines, he steps back. "When I was in high school," he tells her in Russian, "my girlfriend told me I couldn't carry a tune."

"You know what?"

"What?"

"She was right." They laugh uproariously, improvise like crazy.

The unofficial Lida file is in an old Drambuie carton. He showed me what was in all of them several years ago. But yesterday, I was alone, kneeling on the floor of Mac's study, and what I saw in her eyes and in the moist fullness of her lips in this particular photograph was what I saw in Brussels.

She is languid and loose, utterly spent, her head thrown back in a glorious, full-body laugh. Her hair is long and unkempt, unevenly parted down the middle, cheekbones high, collarbone gleaming above the scoop-necked pullover. You can tell she and the photographer just got out of bed. Stieglitz's pictures of Georgia O'Keeffe.

I found another photograph yesterday too, one Mac had never shown me before. I take it out of my bag and prop it against the base of the Steenbeck screen. It's a shiny black-and-white snapshot with a border, three by five inches. "The protagonist's journey is what moves the story forward," I was taught in film school. "In every scene you write, direct, or edit, these are the questions you must ask: What does the protagonist want? What are the obstacles in his way? What does he do to overcome them?" Even in a documentary, we were told, you have to keep the audience wondering what is going to happen next. In this case, the protagonist is a woman, and even in this wrinkled old photograph, there's no mistaking what she wants and how much she wants it.

In a matter of days Mac is spoiled. There are tours of Leningrad, midnight toasts, Lida's undivided attention from the moment he picks her up at the curb outside her office building and they drive to the site she has picked out for the early evening. The theater, the public garden where Pushkin wrote poetry in his bathrobe, the lobby of the Hotel Astoria where Hitler had planned a huge celebration to commence as soon as he took Leningrad, the titanic statue of Catherine the Great in Ostrovsky Square, with her favorites on the pedestal at her feet. There was a woman in the court, Lida tells Mac, whose job was to sleep with men and report on their prowess to Catherine, so she could decide which ones to take.

The days are long but not long enough. They lie utterly still for minutes that seem like hours. She is not sure anymore whether he is inside her or she is inside him, and when she tells him this afterwards, he is aroused all over again. Like a boy of eighteen he needs no more than a word or two, a picture. He comes on her belly, between her lips, in the center of her palm, and she covers her breasts with it, murmuring, laughing, "Goodbye, little girls and boys, goodbye."

But on their sixth night, Mac opens his front door to greet her and she stands there shyly, fists stuffed in the pockets of her jacket, as if she is not sure she is welcome.

"You've come to the right place."

"Excuse me?"

"Come in."

"Thank you."

They are strangers. Since six o'clock this morning they have grown apart. "How are you?"

"Normal." It has half a dozen meanings in Russian—okay, ordinary, proper, acceptable—but it is used most often in greetings in place of "I'm fine." But until tonight when he asked, she had always said, I'm immensely happy at this moment.

"And how are you?" Her "you" tonight is formal.

They have approached her, threatened her. Or maybe he has been wrong about her all along, maybe she is here to offer some confession out of a spy novel: her affection has been a sham. Or: it began as an assignment, but I had no idea it would turn into this.

"I'm fine," Mac answers, and takes her jacket out of her

hands. "Can I get you a drink?" Or maybe the explanation is, as she would say, normal. Ordinary. The oldest explanation in the book. She has come to her senses. She is tired of him.

From her shoulder bag she takes an airmail envelope and holds it out. No return address. In the dim light of the foyer he squints at the postmark. Helsinki.

My darling Lida, I am here on the train and will mail this as soon as I reach Finland. I can't get you out of my mind, even more now than when we met in January. I feel so close to you, I feel we are already married. My parents will be crazy about you, and so will Uli and Sachi, when I tell them, and of course, Bambi. I will ask my parents to breed her so we can have a puppy. Let me know as soon as you can whether I should plan to return at Christmas or whether—

There is no doubt about the identity of the suitor, but Mac skips anyway to the closing. Heinrich. He takes a deep breath, kicks aside a pang of jealousy, kicks it hard, like a soccer ball. "Well. Congratulations." Who is Mac to her anyway? The last to exert a claim on her affections. "Come on in, we'll have a toast." The second-oldest story in the book. A married man just passing through. "I might even have some vodka left." He leads her to the kitchen, he feels like a maître d' new on the job. Doesn't quite believe his own hospitality. "Or we can go out and buy a bottle."

"That's not necessary. If you have a Heineken."

"Coming right up."

"What's all this?"

The kitchen counter is covered with fresh vegetables, on-ions, eggplant, zucchini, tomatoes, and a raw leg of lamb. "I thought we might cook dinner. I'm not sure how to cook a piece of meat like that, but I figured we could—"

"Where did it come from, the *beriozka*? Where else can you buy such—"

"The farmer's market."

"But you must have spent—"

He hands her the beer. "A few kopecks."

"I had sort of forgotten about him," she says, and takes a long swig, "until the letter came."

"Me too."

"Do you know Geneva?"

"I was there once years ago."

"Would I like it?"

Mac opens a bottle of beer for himself, flips off the top, and watches it skitter across the counter. "It's very pretty."

"So is Leningrad."

"In a different way. The scale is much different. Smaller. It doesn't sprawl. And there's a lake on the edge of the city with a great jet of water arcing across it."

"Anything else?"

"The mountains of course. And it's spotless. The streets are so clean you can eat off them."

"Why don't you like it?"

"I don't like it or not, I have very few impressions, I was only there—"

"You make it sound dull."

"I suspect it is dull."

"So I would be a fool to live there?"

"Not at all. If you have a chance to get out, take it. Grab it. If you don't like Geneva, you can leave. Once you're out, you can go wherever you want."

But if that is the sort of the marriage it is going to be, Mac knows they ought not to talk about it here. "Let's go out and have a toast. We'll go to the Finnish bar and buy a bottle of champagne. I told you about the hotel with the hard-currency bar, didn't I?"

"I never thought I would marry someone I don't love."

"But he has such good manners. That's important in a marriage. Good penmanship too. Though that's not as important, unless you plan to spend long periods apart." He is trying to make her laugh, but she is distracted, unmoved, her glance is in the direction of the floor. He reaches for her free hand. "People get married for all sorts of reasons. Come out with me tonight and I'll show you one of them."

She looks up. "What's that?"

"I'll teach you how to jitterbug at the Finnish bar. They have a jukebox." He nestles close to her, he wants to cut down the chances that every word they say will be picked up and transmitted. "Even if you marry, you're not tied to him. If you're unhappy you can leave. You can travel, move to another city, another country. It's not the way it is here, Lida. You can do whatever you please, whenever you please."

But she is unimpressed. He is a salesman at her door hawking Bibles, Polish radios, raffle tickets. Her silence and stiffness alert him to the possibility that what she wants from him is not the truth about Geneva but something more remote. "If things were different, if I weren't married—"

"Did you love your wife when you married her?"

"I thought I did. I suppose I did."

"I would like at least to think that I did too. But with Heinrich—"

"You already married someone you don't love," he whispers.

"That was different."

"Someone you won't even hold hands with."

"It was a favor. Heinrich thinks this is the real thing."

"He'll get over it."

"I wouldn't want to hurt him or his family."

Mac forgets that she is so young, so innocent, that even with all her boldness and charm, this is all she knows, all she can imagine. She thinks nothing of KGB agents lurking in every doorway, but it would be unfathomable cruelty to hurt Heinrich's mother's feelings. The poor guy holds out the globe and she hands it back with an explanation: I don't come by this honestly.

"So tell him the truth," Mac whispers. Does it matter if the KGB hears all this? If she decides she wants to leave, it matters. "Tell him you want to get out. You're tired of whispering. Of being followed, being listened to, of—"

"But I'm not. This is my home. Leningrad is the soul of Russia. Why do you think the people never let it fall to the Germans?"

He would have been no more surprised if she had broken into the "Internationale." Is this for the benefit of the KGB or is this for real?

"France, Holland, Belgium—they fell like dominoes."

She means every word, and though she will not recite Bukharin's crimes or the resolutions adopted by the Third Party Congress, there is a place she will draw the line and wave the flag for the motherland: even the wife of a cheating husband sticks up for him when strangers come around. Maybe it isn't really in her, Mac thinks, to marry someone she doesn't love. Maybe Mac is projecting: he himself would marry a midget if it meant getting out of here. And perhaps there is another reason he wants her to leave so badly: once she is out, she is free to go where she pleases, and it might please her to come to Washington.

"Let's go out," he says again softly, gently. "No toasts, just an ordinary drink."

"What about all this food?"

"The hell with it. We can dance. We can watch the Finns who come over on their one-day visas see the sights of Leningrad from inside a bottle of vodka."

"You think I should practice hanging around with foreigners? So I can get ready for life in Geneva?"

Has she changed her mind? If she has, this isn't the place to question her further. They have said too much already. He lifts his arms and holds her face in his hands. "So I can teach you to jitterbug."

She shakes her head and whispers, "It's a foreign bar, Mac, they won't let me in. You know that."

"Fuck it. Let's go anyway. I was there a few weeks ago, nobody asked to see my passport."

"You look American."

"So do you, in your jeans and clogs. Come on, put on one of my shirts, that'll help."

"It won't work."

"Leave your passport here. If they ask, pretend you don't understand Russian."

"And if they speak to me in English?"

"I'll tell them you're deaf. What's wrong?"

"I'll be right back."

He follows her down the hall to the door of his bedroom, watches as she sits on the edge of the bed and digs a wallet out of her purse. She unclasps the change compartment and removes a strip of lined paper folded over on itself four or five times. It opens like an accordion. She picks up the phone on the nightstand and dials the number she reads from the scrap of paper.

"May I speak to Stazi, please . . . Hey, Stazi, how you doing, pal? . . . No kidding, I was thinking about you too . . . Normal, how about you? . . . Really? . . . I walked by your office the other day, looked up to that little window you showed me once. Where were you? . . . Maybe next time. You know who I saw the other day, you won't believe it— Katya, she's having a baby . . . Already it looks like a basketball under there. Only five months gone . . . Maybe she will but I wouldn't count on it, Stazi, maybe you should bring it up with her husband. He's a nice guy but not a fool . . . Oh, okay, sure, no problem . . . No, just wanted to say hello. So long."

She drops the receiver into the cradle and says nothing. Mac says nothing. Halfway through the conversation, he took a guess at Stazi's identity. And when Lida stands and pushes his carefully folded phone number into the pocket of her jeans, he knows for certain: her friend from high school who works for the KGB. "I wanted to make sure I could still reach him." She chortles. "The little prick."

"I'll get you my shirt and then we'll go dancing."

"Mac, if they contact me, if they ask me questions about you, what should I say?"

"I issue visas in the consulate."

"What else?"

"Anything I say to you, you can repeat." But he knows there are a hundred things he can never tell her. That he was sent here suddenly, asked on a Thursday to leave Washington on Sunday. That there is nowhere in the consulate where one can have a secure conversation, because they haven't finished getting all the Soviet bugs out of the room they used to think was secure. That in the two months he's been here, the KGB has dangled a half dozen bits of bait in his face. The old man who sat at his table in the Evropeiskaya dining room and announced he did undersea research in the Far East. How nice for you, Mac had said, and went on eating his sturgeon and stewed tomatoes. The novice agent who accosted him and Susan the nanny outside the Kirov, and when they declined his invitation for coffee, the poor guy begged them to come to his flat for a drink. Two naval officers, a young army lieutenant, and a leggy woman in an apricot-colored miniskirt who sat next to him one night at the Kirov and was dying to talk during intermission. And of course he can't tell Lida that he might be told any day to pack his bags and get on the next plane out of here. "You can even tell them what I say in my sleep," he said.

The rules here are meant only to keep you off balance, keep you guessing about where the real danger lies. It's everywhere, isn't it? That's what they want you to think. Maybe it's true. But whoever is listening on the headphones, labeling and cataloging the reels of tape—this is the only conclusion they will be able to reach: Lida and Mac are practically starved. She turns to ask about the shirt she will borrow and it is no more than the startling aquamarine of her eyes that draws him across the room. She undoes his pants with one hand and the buttons of her blouse with the other. What thrills him more than any specific sensation is the blunt fact of her desire. She wants this as much as he does. "I'll tell the Komitet you are a genius in bed," she murmurs. "Valedictorian of the class." She kneels and rubs her nipples against his knees, her tongue to the crease of his scrotum. He will tell Babette her name, that he met her in a restaurant, that her father is in the military, but how can he possibly tell her that beneath the eyes of the

secret police, a love affair with every single sigh on tape—
How can he tell his wife that in this country of vast, unspeakable sorrows, where the newsreels of his childhood, the Siege in the dead of winter, play around the clock, he is happier than he has been in years?

SEVEN

▼

At the far end of the Saint-Simon lobby, in the arched entranceway to the bar, waiting for Mac to arrive seventeen years later, Lida is out of focus. Eric zooms in. Close-up of her face. Crystal-clear. She's squinting, and you can see her think: Is that Mac there, with the camera on his shoulder? Can't be. Then she sees him, it must be him, or why does her face swell into a smile? It is the face in the photographs, plus seventeen years and maybe seventeen pounds. But there was beauty to spare in those pictures, and youth. Plenty of surplus. There still is. Her hair is still long, still loose, it falls over the shoulders of her sweater, but it's the eyes that grab hold of you, lighting up the room from atop majestic cheekbones. She opens her arms, wraps them around him, whispers his name. There was no sound, no recording yet, but I heard it clearly. All she said was "Mac," but her whisper was low and husky and commanding, as imposing as the rest of her, and such a surprise to me, his name in her throat that way,

her lips at his ear, that I took a step backwards, as if I had
come upon a pair of lovers I didn't want to disturb.

The embrace is brief. Mac pulls back and holds out his arm
to me. "This is my wife, Kate." Lida pivots and her eyes drop
while my head tilts up. She must be six feet tall in bare feet,
a little taller than Mac. Her smile is immense, resplendent,
even as she looks at me. Eyes the color of Caribbean waters,
traces of perfume that smell like jasmine and roses. I hold out
my hand and she grips it in hers. It's huge, like a man's, and
faintly callused. I think of Soviet stereotypes, farm women
who drive tractors, women as sturdy and overgrown as giant
zucchini born of long summer days in Alaskan latitudes. I
think of all those women who stood up to the Germans for
nine hundred days. Mac hadn't told me she was quite so tall,
and it didn't come through in his snapshots of her. Mostly,
he'd been preoccupied with her face, and now I can see why
for myself.

She turns to Mac and leads him by the elbow from the
lobby into the bar. I have some idea, I don't know where it's
from, that she is married to a laborer, an electrician, a printer,
and traveling on the cheap, a group of friends driving to Belgium and sharing a room in a fleabag owned by a Soviet friend,
an exile from a ruble economy making his way in francs. But
this isn't it. Marble floors, a marble bar top, tables and stools
of fine dark wood with brass details. A European chicness, an
abundance of bright light. We are swept into the bar in the
crush of a small crowd.

"Come, come," she says. "Meet the good friends." Mac
shakes hands with a short, swarthy young man. I shake hands
with him. We shake hands with the bartender. We shake hands
with three or four other people. Are they the friends she traveled here with? They disappear like servants. The rest of the

place is empty, no one but us at the bar or in the booths at our backs. It's almost eleven on a Sunday night, the cab let us off on a deserted street. "Ah, Mac"—she grips his jacketed upper arm, runs her hand, her huge hand, down to his elbow—"I begin look for you seven o'clock in morning. I go in, I ask, 'Mr. MacKenzie?' No. All the time, no. 'Mac-Kenzie?' No. 'MacKenzie?' No. Why not your name is by last hotel where you call to me?"

I had heard Mac speak English to her on the phone, but in my mind, in my imagination, she still speaks only Russian, the way she did when Mac knew her.

"The reservation was in my wife's name," Mac says, but she doesn't seem to hear.

"So, much after the noon, already it's night, I come here and drink. Good friend what owns hotel, he make phone calls, many hotels. Still no achievement. More we drink." She cackles and mimes belting back shot glasses. Her laughter is thick and raucous and unabashed; it carries like gunfire. She strokes Mac's arm again and doesn't let go. Her turquoise eyes don't waver from his. If Eric had pried the camera from her face, he might have gotten a shot of me gaping.

Then she pivots to the camera. "Who you are?" she asks Eric. Her face is alive, her cheeks full and flushed, as if she had a fever of a hundred and two. She must not have noticed the camera before, must not have understood that where we go, it goes. "Maybe we are on CNN?"

"We're just fooling around," Eric says. "You like to fool around?"

"What means fool around?"

Mac says something in Russian, translating.

"*Da*, fool around. I love fool around. Maybe you create movie of my situation?"

"Maybe we will." Eric's voice has acquired a flirtatious lilt. She is juicier than he had any reason to imagine she would be.

"Eric that's enough," I tell him.

"We're just getting started."

"You need drink," Lida says, and motions to the bartender, waving her enormous hand. "He needs drink. He works very much hard. You want wine? Cognac? Vodka?"

"Eric. cut."

"What is cut?"

But he doesn't. He follows Lida down the bar. Mac follows Lida. We are all following Lida. But somewhere off-screen, I reach for Mac's arm myself. And then for hers. "Why don't you two sit down," I say, "and talk."

"What?" Lida says to me. She is not sure what I mean.

I give them each a tiny shove toward the barstools. "Go ahead. Sit and talk. In Russian."

Permission. Now she gets it. Permission to reminisce. "Thank you very much wife of Mac," she says in one long breath.

"Don't mention it."

They slip onto stools and I glance around the bar for a telephone. Why not let them talk? Her English is serviceable, but I know they have plenty to say that can't be said in the present tense, and the sooner they say it, the sooner we can leave. I will call my assistant in New York to check for messages, any news from the crew we're meeting in Turkey. But as I lean forward to ask the bartender about a phone, I catch her reflection in the mirror on the back wall of the bar. Nothing extraordinary to behold: a man and a woman, drinks that move from the countertop into their hands, up to their mouths. She's talking in an ordinary voice, in a language I can't understand, but I'm mesmerized. It's as if I've discovered the Princess of Wales in the checkout line at Duane Reade. I cannot believe she's really there, and I cannot take my eyes off her. I slip onto the barstool beside Mac and watch in the mirror.

"A drink?" the bartender says.

Her hushed Russian is unfamiliar, guttural, full of *zh*'s and *gd*'s, not a single word is recognizable. A foreign film with no subtitles. But I understand perfectly what I am witnessing: they haven't missed a beat, they have picked up in the middle of a seventeen-year-old conversation put on hold by forces beyond their control, and I have just seen those years collapse before my eyes, like a high-rise building rigged for demolition with explosives. In a matter of seconds the entire structure is gone.

"Would you like a drink?"

"Whiskey."

The night he left Leningrad, they exchanged presents. He gave her a pair of purple gloves bought at Gostiny Dvor, and when he drove away in that hour of darkness between midnight and one, he could see her wave in his rearview mirror, waving with both hands, the purple gloves and the rest of her disappearing into the blackness within seconds.

"Your drink," the bartender says. His English is accented but not heavily, and out of the corner of my eye I see him lingering, unsure of whether to interrupt my gaping. I am the serpent and she is the snake charmer. "What's happening?" he asks finally.

"Excuse me?"

"What is this movie you are making?"

"It's nothing." But my voice sounds reedy and unconvincing, and whatever this is, anyone watching can see that it is not nothing.

"So perhaps you are English?" he says.

"American."

"You are a student of cinema?"

I shake my head and turn back to her. She is speaking louder now, and I hear a disturbing insistence in her voice, or maybe it is only that I am so unfamiliar with the language that everything she says sounds urgent. I belt back a mouthful of whiskey, closing my eyes, and when I open them, Mac has turned to me. "How you doing?"

"Fine," I mumble, I lie. But what is the truth? That I had no idea she would be so tall, so beautiful, so breathtakingly present?

He leans closer to me. "My Russian is very rusty. I can't understand a lot of what she's saying."

Is he apologizing or just staying in touch? "Oh."

"Another beer?" the bartender asks him.

"I'm okay for now."

Then he turns back to Lida as Eric roams the bar shooting everything in sight, a trigger-happy tourist with a video camera. "Eric"—I wave to get his attention—"that's enough."

"This is good, Kate."

"How much film have you gone through?"

"We're in good shape. Let it roll."

I swallow another mouthful of whiskey and let it roll.

I could have insisted he stop, I know I could have. He knew it too. He must have understood, even if I didn't yet, even if I didn't until this moment, that there was something taking place I would want a record of, something I'd need to take home and study. Was it this tableau of the three of us at the bar—Lida and Mac catching up on all these years, and me staring? I run it back two or three times. Picture without sound. We look, listen, stare, raise and lower our drinks in uneven patterns. There is nothing much to conclude, except that she and Mac are so steeped in each other that they are oblivious to the camera, and I am so gripped by her presence, by her hold on my husband, that I am oblivious to everything else. What was I doing there, gaping like a half-wit? Is this what Eric wanted me to see, or do I give him too much credit? Maybe all he wanted was what I wanted: to keep looking at Lida.

Then the Steenbeck screen goes white. I've come to the end of the roll.

It was in those minutes at the bar, when Eric changed mags, that I remembered I had forgotten the sound and reached into my bag for the cassette player. I placed the recorder on the bar and unwound the mike cord as I picked up a sound I could not place. I looked over at Mac, about to ask, "What's that noise?" when I saw the answer. Tears streamed down Lida's cheeks. The sounds were those of a woman trying to keep from crying. Mac's hand reached up and cupped the side of her face. He ran his thumb against her cheekbone, his eyes squinted in sympathy, and I felt my bones turn to water, to sand. She kept trying to talk, the words were repetitive, rhythmic. I thought I heard the word "mama." Mac's eyes were still squinting, his hand still cradling her face. Mama, I heard her say again. Had her mother died? Was she telling him about when her mother died? My poor mama, she must have been saying. When she died, I said, Mama, I will miss you so.

"Are you American?"

Lida lowered her eyes and pulled a Kleenex from her jacket pocket as Mac's hand dropped away from her face.

"Are you American?"

The voice came from behind, and I realized then it was

meant for me. I twisted my neck until I could see into the booth at my back: it was one of the men we had shaken hands with before, a friend of Lida's, but now there was an unctuous, pitying smile stretched across his face. "For how long are you in Brussels?"

"Overnight."

"Pardon?"

"Overnight."

"Why so short a time in our city?" He looked to be twenty-five or thirty, a slender, light-skinned Indian or Arab with a starched white shirt and a black tie, flicking cigarette ashes into a saucer.

"We got a cheap fare coming through Brussels on our way to Turkey." Hanging on the wall over his table I noticed a small framed print, a Paul Delvaux, naked women hovering by train tracks, immense hot-pink ribbons in their hair and stiff, shattered looks on their faces. I was not about to tell this man, this friend of Lida's, how expensive our fare had just become. But of course he could see for himself.

"You are on holiday?" Yes, he felt sorry for me. He thought that if I was distracted by small talk, I wouldn't dwell on the scene from *Peyton Place* I had just witnessed at my elbow.

"No," I said. It was all I cared to say. I swiveled back to the bar and resumed my watch. Gaping at Lida. Gaping at Mac, who was gaping at Lida, who was no longer crying. I see it again here on Fifteenth Street. There is nothing extraordinary to see. A woman in an angora sweater and dark blazer, a man in a turtleneck, a pause while she sips her wine, laughs at something Mac has said, and motions to the bartender for a refill. Nothing extraordinary except the look on Mac's face. I became a documentary filmmaker because of the look on his face right there, because it is spontaneous, unrehearsed, unscripted, and so full of feeling. It's all in his eyes. He is in Leningrad with Lida, in bed with Lida, at a candlelit table for two, except that I happen to be sitting next to him at a bar in Brussels. And the camera is rolling. Every frame is real life, in spades. I am changing shape, becoming someone else, like Alice in Wonderland or Gregor Samsa. I am Lida waving to Mac, growing smaller and smaller in his rearview mirror. Goodbye, little girls and boys, goodbye.

I slid off my barstool and caught the bartender's eye. "Where's the ladies' room?"

"Pardon?"

I remembered I was in Europe. "The toilet."

He pointed to the door at the far end of the bar. "Inside the door, on the right."

I entered a narrow, dimly lit corridor ten or twelve feet long. There was a fire door on my left with a horizontal metal rod about hip level that would release the door, a pay phone on the wall, one door for "Hommes," one for "Femmes," and several others, unmarked. I could have slipped out right there, swung my hip against the metal rod and left. All I had really wanted was to get a look at her and leave them to their lunch in Paris in three weeks. Through the door I heard Lida's voice and the raucous blare of her laughter every minute or two. She laughed the way waves break, with an imprecise predictability, and a great *boom*. I stared for a long time at the pay phone. There was a single slot at the top of the box but not a word about how much money it needed or how to reach an operator. I picked it up anyway and listened to a long, unremitting beep. I could call my friend Nan in New York, if I could figure out how. Go out there, she'd say, and tell Mac the reunion's over. Tell him you're as understanding as the next liberated woman, but Anna Karenina is more than you bargained for.

But Nan's simple, straightforward advice wasn't what I needed. I needed the patience to sit through this, because I knew he wanted to tell her what had happened at the end, things he couldn't have written in a letter or said over unsecured phones, and if I cut him off tonight, he would find another time. That was when I noticed the silence. I listened for Lida's laughter, but heard nothing. Many, many minutes of nothing, which must have meant that Mac was talking and she was listening. If I could stand by the phone for another fifteen or twenty minutes, as still as the naked women in Paul Delvaux's paintings, as still as the frozen characters in the bank vault in *The Twilight Zone* of my childhood, this would be over. I paced, I glanced at the phone, I decided to tell Mac I was going for a walk. I'd be back in half an hour.

I pulled open the door to the bar and was surprised by the innocence of what I saw: they were talking quietly at the other end of the room. As I approached, about to tell Mac my plans, I heard him speaking English, softly, not looking at her but at the almost empty beer glass he rolled between his palms. I had come in at the end of another story I know inside out, another story Mac told me in the first weeks of our affair, one I would never interrupt. ". . . it was over very fast. That's what his friends told me, and the man who led the tour. The car came out of nowhere, and Sam went flying. The irony—" Surely he knows the word "irony" is beyond Lida's English; he doesn't seem to care, and she is polite enough not to ask what it means. "The terrible irony is that the bicycle barely got a scratch. It was brand-new. He'd had his eye on it for a year. He never asked me for it. He was saving up his allowance and money from a job after school. When he graduated, I gave it to him and sent him on a tour through Oregon and Washington with a bunch of kids his age. They were going sixty, seventy miles a day, sleeping in National Parks, swimming in the rivers. He had just mailed me a postcard the morning of the accident, telling me he was having a terrific time. But by the time I got it— He was such a sweet boy. The kids on the tour, they loved him. Some of them still write to me." Mac looked over at Lida, almost surprised to see her there; he gets lost in this story, he forgets there's someone listening. "I see so many teenagers who are mean to other kids, rude to adults, or just uncomfortable with them. My kids were never like that. They were always curious about my friends, always interested in other people."

"When you tell to me on phone, I am not understand. I think he have maybe can-ker."

"He was fine. Big, healthy, strong. It's been very difficult for Polly. For all of us."

Lida nodded, lifted her glass, and drank, for once at a loss for words. People never know what to say next and you can tell how uncomfortable they feel having gotten Mac to talk about it in the first place, having asked one innocent question too many. Sometimes they apologize and sometimes they try to change the subject, and someone once said, "You must feel so guilty, sending him on that trip," but mostly people squirm for a few seconds, like Lida did, and wait for the moment to pass as they throw up invisible walls between Mac and themselves, between his children and theirs, his tragedy and their own good fortune.

"Today is his birthday."

"Oh, Mac."

"I used to carry him like this." Mac opened his arms wide

as if he were holding a basket of laundry. "But now it feels more like he's on my back. A papoose. I forget sometimes that he's there." He kept his eyes on the bartop, but even when they started to fill with tears, not many, she did not do what I had feared, she did not try to comfort him, not so much as a hand over his. But I would have understood if she had, it is what you would do if you had known of this child when he was four. Mac turned to me. "Do you have the photographs?"

I reached into my bag, passed them down, and Mac handed them to Lida. "This is Polly almost two years ago with her boyfriend, they were camping in Colorado. She looks just like her mother." Lida nodded, though there was no expression on her face. She was looking at a snapshot of a stranger. Then she turned to the picture of Sam when he was seventeen, caught by surprise at the breakfast table. There's a sweet glint in his eye as he shovels a forkful of French toast into his mouth. Another snapshot of a stranger. Our apartment in New York is full of them, and sometimes it seems that the place is haunted, shrouded in grief that will be ours for life, though Sam was never mine.

Lida handed back the pictures and I dropped them into my bag. "I don't work for the government anymore; I said that on the phone, didn't I?" I looked around the room for Eric as I heard Mac explain his work to her. ". . . refugees from everywhere . . . It's mostly church groups who call me for help . . . I don't have to be there all the time, but I do what I can . . . Latin Americans, Haitians, now and then I get a call from Eastern Europe . . . The other day a colleague called about the situation in Yugoslavia. It doesn't look good, does it?"

I slid off the barstool and wandered back to the darkened corridor with my shoulder bag, pulling a telephone credit card from my wallet. I should have phoned my assistant from our hotel when we arrived, and there might be instructions on the back of the card. I picked up the receiver and held the card in front of my nose, trying to catch a sliver of light. There was a hand on my back. Mac. Of course. We were going to leave. I turned my head.

It was the pest from the bar, the man in the booth who had wanted to distract me with small talk.

"What do you want?"

"Are you trying to make a phone call? Can I help?"

"No. Thank you." I listened for his retreating steps.

"I am in doubt you can call international from this phone. Do you mind if I ask you a few questions?"

I replaced the receiver and turned to him, more annoyed than curious. "What kind of questions?"

"I can't do it here. I work in the hotel. I need to sit near the lobby, in case someone comes in. Would you come there with me?"

I did not move.

"Come," he said, not harshly.

"Where?"

"In this room—" He motioned to an unmarked door. "I just want to talk."

There were no questions I cared to answer, nothing I had to say to this man, but I followed him through the door with a kind of idle curiosity, and nothing better to do. We were in a large, plush sitting room that led back to the lobby, heading for a pair of stuffed chairs at the far end, and a shiny walnut coffee table arrayed with brochures about Brussels. He motioned for me to take a seat, and I wished then I had said no to all of it. There was something cagey in his gestures, as if this were an interview for a job already promised to someone else. He held out a pack of cigarettes. I shook my head. We had a view of the front desk and the small foyer on the other side of which was the entrance to the bar.

"Is that man your husband?"

"What man?"

"At the bar. Talking to Lida."

"Yes."

"Oh." It was a long, melodic, very significant oh. "I'm a translator," he said. "I've been many times to Russia."

"And?" What had he overheard? Surely he didn't mean to tell me about Mac's work helping refugees.

"I'm not married, so when I go out with a woman, I don't have the same responsibilities. It doesn't matter as much how I treat a woman. Do you understand what I'm saying?"

"Not really."

"Do you speak Russian?"

"No."

"None?"

"A few words."

"I see." There was a pained look on his face, like that of a doctor who must deliver bad news, and that was when I understood. He was poised to tell me something that would crush me, this stranger, this smarmy hotel clerk, this friend of Lida's. I was not going to hear it, I would keep him from saying another word. I leaned forward as if I were about to shake my finger at him. "What's going on in there"—I wanted to sound tough, but my voice, high up in my throat, gave me away—"is more complicated than I have any interest in telling you. Do you understand me?"

"I think I do."

Mac was talking politics, refugees, the ramifications of the collapse of the Soviet Empire. What this creep meant, what he objected to, was that it was rude for Mac to be engaged, so engaged, in a conversation I didn't understand. All right, it was a bit rude. I conceded that. But he didn't know what I knew. He didn't know that three months after Mac returned to Washington, the security people asked for all the letters she had written him, the gifts she gave him, the photographs he took of her. They showed the pictures to the Marine guards at the Embassy in Moscow and the Consulate in Leningrad. Do you know this woman? Take your time, have a good look. Here's another shot. Recognize her? Has she approached you? Look again. Is she a spy? Is she a hooker? Does she fuck for money or does she fuck for the motherland? I turned to the hotel clerk. "I knew they would be speaking Russian. It's not a surprise to me."

"Of course." He was disappointed he couldn't rattle me, sorry I had recovered so swiftly from his assault. "So you are making a movie?"

"In Istanbul."

"But what about here? That man with the camera, he said—"

How could I explain what the man with the camera was doing? I had no idea myself. "If you want to know what he's doing, ask him."

"I'd rather talk to you. You make movies. What kind of movies?"

"Different kinds."

"Like *Pretty Woman*?"

"Not that kind."

"Can I see them in Brussels?"

"I doubt it."

"You have them on tape? Video?"

"Of course."

"So maybe you will send me one."

I looked at him. I must have looked at him very sharply.

"Why such a problem?"

"I don't have money to spend on things like that."

"No problem. You send me movie and I send you money.
I write down my address. Come with me."

He led me into the lobby, to the front desk, and took out
a hotel calling card from a drawer. Belhaloumi Jebel, he wrote
on it, Please Send Your Movie And I Will Pay. An Arab who
speaks Russian, an Arab who cannot mind his own business.
Suddenly Mac appeared at my side. "Where were you? I've
been looking all over."

I was shocked to see him there. Or maybe shocked that he
looked just like himself, not the stranger Belhaloumi Jebel had
led me to believe he'd become. "I was talking to this man.
He wants me to send him one of my films."

Mac ignored him and opened his arm to me, leading me
back into the bar. I assumed we were about to leave, and he
was taking me there to say goodbye.

I see myself smiling in the next shot, inching toward the
semicircular booth where Lida sat with her flushed cheeks and
her ardent, toothy smile. She was full of my husband, that
accounted for her glee. But I was smiling only because I was
sure this meant our visit was almost over. I was sure we were
coming up on Act Three. I held out my hand to her. We had
shaken when we were introduced, and I'd shake her hand again
on my way out. "Sit down with us," Mac said. "Let's not leave
so soon."

My arm dangled in the air and Lida laughed at the sight of it. Or was it the sight of Mac's wife caught out that she found so hilarious?

I breathe deeply and look at my watch. I've only seen twenty minutes of footage. I am in New York but my insides are in Brussels, rumbling, churning, I am about to be operated on. It could be can-ker, it could be something worse. Mac and I are tuned to each other like seismographs. He notices every one of my tremors and trembles and sighs. He can distinguish a 3.1 from a 3.2 without consulting the readouts. But the equipment wasn't working right in Brussels, and I'm still not sure how to fix it.

EIGHT

I was on the qui vive.

An expression I first heard from Mac and never had occasion, until that night, to use. Same phrase, same state of alert, same woman.

"I was on the qui vive at all times," Mac had told the State Department investigators in Washington the fall of 1974. "I wasn't naïve or stupid about this. I didn't galavant around Leningrad befriending Soviet citizens. I was sensitive to the fact that she could have been contacted and recruited. That she could be turned. But from the way we met, I was positive she hadn't been planted on me, unless they had the whole of Leningrad carpeted. Unless every woman in the city was under orders to entice me."

"What would you say if we told you she was working for the KGB?"

"She's a terrific actress."

"That's all?"

"She never asked about my job, and I never volunteered a thing. As I told you last week, as soon as I arrived in Leningrad, I asked Gary Tucker for a security briefing. He told me there wasn't a secure room in the consulate, and that was the extent of my guidance. I made a point of introducing Lida to people at the consulate, so the KGB couldn't blackmail me, and no one took me aside and said that fraternizing with Soviets was against the rules. If I had been told it was, I assure you, I would have complied."

"But what if she *was* working for them? What would you say to that?"

Mac started to shrug. Really, the idea was unfathomable—she cared less about matters of state, any state, than most Americans—but if they insisted on an answer, and they did, he would oblige them. "Thanks for the memories," he said finally.

The investigator's jaw dropped.

When he first told me the story, in his bed, mine did too. "That's all you said, 'Thanks for the memories'?"

"I hadn't done anything wrong. I asked for a security briefing my first morning at the consulate and they didn't think it was important enough to give me."

"But don't you think you were operating a little close to the edge, I mean—"

"If anyone there had told me not to fraternize with Soviet citizens, I wouldn't have. I wasn't trying to test the system, believe me, but in the absence of any instructions, I used my judgment. And I don't think I judged wrong."

"It's a wonder they didn't fire you. For failure to repent."

"They tried."

Sitting between the two of them that night in Brussels, I was as suspicious of her motives, and of his, as the Feds had been.

"Before yesterday, I not know nothing about Mac. Not know if he alive. I am all the time wonder. You know, in Moscow, we have now McDonald's, but all the time, so long lines. Close by, statue of Pushkin. Russian people, they say, 'Even Pushkin have to wait for Big Mac!' That's you. Big Mac." She tips her chin and laughs her raucous bray.

Mac is trying not to smile, not to get it.

"I tell to you on phone, I am big businesswoman now. I make deals all kinds business what wants Russian people. I have good car and cellular phone. You want I call you"—she explodes with laughter even before the punchline—"and us make little business?"

The cassette recorder is in the middle of the table—Eric must have moved it there—and Belhaloumi Jebel is nuzzling up to Lida, bending at the knee, trying to push into the booth beside her. She cocks her head and hurls him a look that says, "Get lost."

"I can't sit down?"

"No."

"Not even for—"

"No. Bye-bye."

Then she turns to me with a bold smile, but at the bottom of my field of vision, there's something lunging toward me. Her huge hand has clutched my forearm. I straighten up, feel the power in her fingers, and press myself into the seatback, avoiding the end of a knife. Is this a challenge to arm wrestle or something more deadly? "I know what you feel." Her voice is low and throaty and theatrical. Greta Garbo. Bela Lugosi.

"We are womens together. We understand same situations very good, yes?"

But she does not wait for my answer. She removes her hand and turns to Mac directly across the booth. My head bobs from one of them to the other, I am watching for the next serve. "It is not big secret. I love him. Even now, such old man. I have good joke, good Russian joke. American woman, France woman, Russian woman. American woman she say, I like young guys because they nervous, don't know nothing. France woman she say, I like middle age because pratique, know all about sex. Russian woman she say, I like very, very old man. They say, You stupid, you crazy! She say, No, it's very good because every time, he think maybe it's last time, he makes so good sex!" A peal of rowdy laughter. Mac's lips are curling into a faint smile. A layer of modesty. A torrent of pleasure beneath it. He cannot take his eyes off her, this man who does not even flirt with other women at parties.

"I not know if you live," she murmurs. "Don't know nothing. But when Susan tells to me she will gets married and I make visit to States, I tell to her, Now I look for Mac. Now is time. 'Lida, it is not normal. Don't be crazy.' But I am crazy, always little bit crazy, and much spontane. I phone to Susan in Chee-cago three o'clock today. 'Any word yet?' she ask. 'No, not yet.' 'Where he can be?' 'Who can say?' Then tonight, you call."

"But we were supposed to see you in Paris," I tell her, "in three weeks."

"I am not understand."

Is she playing dumb or is what she understands much more limited than what she is capable of expressing?

"Didn't you and Mac agree we would come to Paris on our way home from—"

"Why not Brussels? I make for you easy. I have car, we make drive. It's no problem."

Is she stubborn or cagey, or is the map of her universe really one without fixed boundaries? Now that she is free to go where she pleases, she does it every chance she gets.

"How did you find me in New York?" Mac asks, eager to change the subject. "In all the commotion, I forgot to ask you."

"I ask to Susan, Please call operator in Washington. My English not so good, I cannot. 'No, Lida, forget,' she tells to me, 'don't be crazy no more.' I make for her to call. You no live in Washington no more, but she find name of Polly. Of course I remember name of childrens . . ."

Suddenly Lida turns to me. "I have good husband. But problems. Mac have the problems too. Both many problems. Good man, my husband, but he want me home, all the time clean, clean, clean, like hospital."

"Can I get you another round?" It's the voice of the bartender, off-screen.

I shake my head. I want to get out of here, and I'm trying to transmit that message to Mac.

"Drink for me," Lida says, and downs what's left in her glass. "By all the means."

"I'm fine." Mac holds up his hand, waving away more.

"No, you are *not* fine," she corrects, she intones. She has become the resident expert on the state of my husband's mental health. Knows just what he needs. Anesthesia. An open marriage. A trial separation. "Give him drink."

"No, thanks. I really don't want another."

"What is matter? It is not normal."

"I'm getting too old. Tell me about your business."

"Many joint venture, all the time phone rings. I am buy

trucks in France and send baby food to St. Petersburg. I meet
with Sobchak, send four trucks baby cloth-ess, baby toys, and
medical. For this, I charge nothing, because it touch me
here"—she taps her hand to her chest—"childrens what need
cloth-ess and food. But I have big repute. People call to me.
'Lida, we want sell umbrellas in Siberia. Who to call, what
to say?' 'Lida, we go to Tashkent for to make cars. You come
for to translate and make deal with Russians what no one
understands.' A friend in Paris, he call to me, he say, 'You
like dirty phone call?' 'What is happening? I no like.' 'No,
Lida, no, we made sex phone in Russia. You pay for to listen
to girl. Us make lots money. Every call, fifty-fifty joint venture.' So I think, Hmmm, not so bad idea, but too soon.
'Raphael, two years, we make rich!' " She roars with laughter.
She's drunk, she's high, nearly out of control, and I seem to
be the only one here who minds.

Eric squats and brings the camera closer to the table, getting
a tight close-up of her feverish face. She looks into the lens
and crosses her eyes. Then she turns back to Mac. "Please to
tell me what is movie of which we are actors."

Mac turns and opens his hand, presenting me. It is, after
all, my show. Or it was when it started.

I hear a long silence on the sound track, and I see myself
on the screen staring at her dumbfounded. But I'm not speechless, I'm only trying to keep myself from blurting out everything
on the tip of my tongue. You're good material. You're dy-
namite. You're trying to blow my marriage to bits. Or is this
Russian hospitality? "It's about the evolution of *perestroika* and
glasnost into the postcoup industrial psychology."

She looks at me dimly. My English has devolved into something like hers. "I am not understand," she tells me, and this time I believe her. "Why not you make movie about us romance? KGB, CIA, all the time little men listen, listen." She turns to Mac as the bartender slides a fresh glass of wine onto the table. "How is English of *glasnost?*"

"The word is openness."

Whisper, he told her in his bedroom in Leningrad, the place is bugged.

It's fun to whisper, she whispered.

There may even be cameras, he said.

Oh, good. I love getting my picture taken.

"How long have you lived in Paris?" Mac asks.

"Two years. Before we live South of France."

"Did you work when you lived there?" I ask.

"No. My girl, Sonya, eight years, too young for mama what works when we live in Nice." She is talking to me but looking at Mac. "All the family now, we have club, we play tennis. Sonya, we study her to swim competition sport. Everyone know me at club. I am big businesswoman. I make good contact, good deals." Emma Bovary with a Dustbuster and tennis racket, her eye on the Siberian tourist trade. Mac is enchanted. He is back in Leningrad with Lida, his rebellious Russian beauty, the daring, darling daughter of the Soviet general whom he spied on from a potato field when he was twenty-one.

Now she is waving to someone over Mac's shoulder. A new member of the cast, a man. She calls him over and introduces us. This is Vladimir, one of the friends with whom she drove up from Paris, a very good friend from university in Leningrad. He is blond and lean, with a face that looks as if it has seen a lot of bar fights or the inside of a labor camp, a crooked nose, and a tear-shaped scar beneath one eye. I wonder how much Lida has told him about my husband. She gets up and motions for him to sit with us, to slide in next to me, so that she does not have to.

"Where you go?" she asks him.

"We have big dinner with Uri's friend, Jean-Louis. What is this here?" He touches the cassette player.

"Look," Lida tells him, pointing to Eric and the camera. "Is Komitet," she whispers but loud enough for us to hear, a mock-whisper, "in time of *glasnost*." Vladimir turns to her in horror. She holds his gaze and then bursts out laughing.

I look at my watch and imagine we have wandered into the heart of Buñuel's *Exterminating Angel*. We came for a drink only to discover that there is no way out.

"She makes movie of *glasnost*," Lida tells Vladimir, pointing to me. "But better idea I give her, us romance in Leningrad. Mac, Lida, CIA, KGB. Good story, no?"

"Well," Mac says, "it's getting late. We've all had a long day." I can hear myself sigh. "Why don't Kate and I come back and visit tomorrow morning? How's ten o'clock for you?"

"Tomorrow?" Lida says. "You stay tomorrow?"

"I thought you knew."

"But we go to Bruges, for tourism, early morning. Then we drive to Paris in the night."

"We'll be here until seven in the evening." Mac still doesn't notice that I'm glowering at him, more stunned by his invitation than Lida must be. "I was hoping we could spend some more time together."

"Oh. But how I will— If friends go to Bruges with car, how we make reunion?" She and Vladimir begin speaking Russian in hushed voices. I turn to Mac, about to tell him that we have plans for tomorrow, when Lida announces, "We make achievement. Vladimir and Uri, they go in morning to Bruges and—" She finishes the sentence in a flurry of Russian and ends with the English word "okay?"

"That sounds fine," Mac says. I turn to him, my eyes alive with fear. What did he just agree to? "Kate and I will pick you up in the morning."

But surely he knows I won't sit through another round of this. It's as if Lida knows it too. She gazes at him with longing lifted right from the silver screen. "So we spend all the day together " she murmurs. "You drink all the afternoon and tell me secrets."

He smiles shyly.

"We have wonderful day together." She is already there, in the middle of tomorrow. "Breakfast, then art museum, then we go—"

"Cut," I say.

She turns to me. "What is cut?"

I motion to Eric with my index finger to come here. The camera is still rolling. He slides off the barstool, head still hunched over the camera, one eye hard against the eyepiece, the other squeezed shut, and steps toward me, so close that the fluttering purr of the film moving through the gate is almost at my ear. I look straight into the deep purple glow of the lens, and I know he can read my lips, he has heard me say these words at the end of every day we shoot: "Roll it out. That's a wrap." Then I snap my fingers to sync the sound. Then I turn to Lida. "That's cut."

"What she did say?" Lida asks Mac.

"She's tired," Mac explains, and stands to let me out of the booth. Another few syllables of diplomacy. Count on Mac to make nice to foreigners. Count on Mac to airbrush an occasional translation, to buy us all tickets for the seashore in the middle of a hurricane.

I am looking for my leather jacket, I think I left it on a barstool, or tossed it into one of the empty booths. I slip from one booth to the next and find it folded on the edge of a banquette near the entrance to the bar. I turn to put it on, facing Mac and Lida as they say good night. "See you tomorrow," he says with his back to me, "at ten." I slip my arms into the sleeves as Mac bends forward to kiss Lida's cheek. I take two or three steps toward them. I will shake her hand. I will do the polite thing, the correct thing. There is a reason, I tell myself, for etiquette. It's so that you always know what to do next. It's almost over. He kisses her cheek, pulls back, and I hear her say, "Is dot *all?*" so loudly that the bartender looks up.

She wants more than a good-night kiss, and Mac is so accommodating, so generous to foreigners in distress, so eager to dress everyone's wounds. I whirl around, away from them, and fly through the lobby, out the heavy glass door that leads to the street, so I am not there to witness what happens next. I need air. It's cold out and drizzly and I have stepped into the slipstream of a car powered on diesel fuel. I am standing up, moving one foot in front of the other in the usual way. I can walk a straight line, count backwards from a hundred, tell you who's President and my mother's maiden name, but I'm reeling.

What does the protagonist want?

Will she be thwarted in getting what she wants? If so, how?

Whisper, he told her, the place is bugged.

Oh, good, I love getting my picture taken.

There's an image I can't put out of my mind, that high-rise building rigged with explosives. It implodes in five seconds, falls in on itself, crashes to the ground in a million pieces, as sure as a woman fainting. In a matter of seconds, the entire structure is gone.

NINE

▼

I don't remember where we are when she tells me this story. Let's say, the kitchen table after everyone else has gone to sleep. It could be that Walter Cronkite has moved to another building, or maybe he never lived in the building my father used to watch through the binoculars, but we are where we were, and they are still married. I imagine us sitting at the white Formica table, in a sea of royal-and-baby-blue-flowered wallpaper with kelly-green accessories: the wooden shutters, the napkin holder, the shiny plastic placemats with scalloped edges. The only room in the apartment given this level of attention. They gussied it up, then ran out of money.

I am fourteen or fifteen when she tells me the story of her wedding night. Or eleven or twelve—it was that kind of family, an abundance of lies and secrets, not much in the way of discretion. Or it may be that people with so many things to conceal don't have the energy left over for decorum.

"Your father must have paid a fortune for the room we had,

the bridal suite overlooking the falls. It was really something
to stare down into that explosion of water. Of course it didn't
look much like water. Looked more like a sheet of white ice
plunging straight down into the center of the earth. It didn't
look at all like the window I had designed for Hutzler's wedding
season display: Niagara in cotton balls."

She still smokes when she tells me this story, and there are
still martinis in the evening and quite a few on weekends,
beginning with Bloody Marys for brunch. The liquor store
around the corner delivers and runs a tab. This block of
Seventy-fifth between Second and Third is our small town,
our village, and the retarded son of the man who owns the
dry cleaner, our own village idiot. One afternoon when I went
in to pick up a wool skirt and we were alone, he grabbed my
breast, not much thicker then than a slice of bread. I never
told anyone, it would have been excruciating to call attention
to my body that way, to make it a subject of inquiry and
controversy, but I still have a distinct memory of the way it
felt, his hand clutching my sweater at the place where a breast
should have been, and my shock.

"We stood hand-in-hand at our window that first night talking about what we'd do tomorrow. Take the *Maid of the Mist*
down into the river, wearing those little yellow slickers and
rain hats. Go on a tour of the caves. And shop. You used to
be able to get Hudson Bay blankets for ten dollars apiece. But
that was tomorrow, and tonight— Well, I had the usual ex-
pectations. I knew I wouldn't enjoy it the first time, I knew
you weren't supposed to. It can be years before a woman feels
one ounce of pleasure—you know that, don't you? So that
wasn't what surprised me, the pain. What surprised me was
when he got up afterwards and put on his jacket and pants.
'What are you doing?' 'Getting dressed.' 'How come?' 'I can't

go down to the bar in my birthday suit, can I?' 'Do you want
company?' 'Sure, why not?' But he didn't mean it, I could
hear that in his voice, and I wasn't going to tag along where
I wasn't wanted. I stayed in the room and he left. I was asleep
when he got back, don't ask how I managed to drift off in that
condition. We never talked about it. I mean, he came back.
It wasn't like he abandoned me. What more was there to say?"

Why did she tell me this?

Why did she tell me, several years later, during the months
of rancor before they divorced, "Last night your father told
me that he wanted to leave ten years ago, when we lived in
Oceanside Gardens, but he didn't because he felt sorry for
me"?

They must have been her warnings, her bulletins from the
front: This is marriage, these are men. Don't forget the mad
money.

Or her motivation might have been more selfish: she had
no one else to talk to late at night, and I have always been a
good listener. It's what people call you when they notice you
don't interrupt and you remember mountains of detail of no
particular consequence, and you hardly ever say anything
about yourself.

"How about some dinner?" It was Mac's voice behind me, his
hand on my back as I stood under the canopy of Lida's hotel
watching the billows of my breath. I've read that in Siberia
your breath freezes into ice dust and falls to the ground; the
Siberians call the sound it makes the whisper of stars. I think
it surprised me that I was still alive.

I started down the sidewalk without looking at Mac or Eric
but felt them follow me. "I would have signed up for the CIA

myself," Eric said, "if somebody had told me about the girls.
What were they like in Vietnam?"

"Shorter," Mac said brusquely. "Kate, do you want some
dinner?"

"It's twelve-thirty."

"It's only six-thirty in New York," Eric said, "or seven-thirty.
Come on, the night is young and the beer in Brussels is terrific.
There's an all-night bar a few blocks from here."

"You want to go for a beer?" Mac asked me.

"No, I don't want a beer."

"What do you want to do?"

"Why don't we try Velcro wall-jumping. That's supposed
to be a kick."

I could hear Mac sigh at my sarcasm. "Let's just go back
to the hotel," he said.

"Fine "

"You two do that," Eric said. "I'm going to look for some
nightlife. Mind taking this with you?" He handed Mac the
camera and me the flight case that held the mags of film.
"You've got the cassette player?" Mac nodded. I had forgotten
completely about it. "See you in the morning." Eric waved
and took off up the empty street, zipping up his leather jacket
against the powdery winter rain.

"There's a cab."

Mac cradled the camera on his lap as he would a cat or a
child, holding it steady as we took a sharp right onto a wide
boulevard. I had taken the equipment to Lida's hotel as armor,
or maybe it was a sort of weapon, to get even with Mac for
welcoming her into our lives with such open arms. The city
whizzed past us, grand, unfamiliar, awash in drizzle and yellow light, a melancholy backdrop to our silence. The camera

had ended up an encumbrance, a quirky conversation piece, like an old pinball machine that doesn't work: How quaint that you bother collecting things like this. Or maybe it became only another vehicle for Lida's ardor: Hey, make a movie about *us*, Mac, me, and the KGB. I had no idea where we were, but over there was a park, orderly rows of bare trees with a low stone wall surrounding them. Beyond that tall gate, a towering neoclassical building, a museum or palace in the glare of a circle of floodlights. And between us was this woman who had careened into our lives the way crazy people drive onto sidewalks at fifty miles an hour.

Mac was the first to speak. "What did that guy want?"

"What guy?"

"The one you were talking to in the lobby when I came looking for you."

"He just asked about the film I'm making. In Istanbul. He wants me to send him some of my films."

"Are you going to?"

"Of course not."

The street narrowed, the springs of our seat made tiny squeals as we bounced over cobblestone. It did not occur to me to tell Mac the truth, I was too sure the hotel clerk had heard something not meant for my ears, and I had heard enough of that in the last ten minutes of our visit.

"So what did you think?" Mac asked, as if we had just come from a movie.

"Obviously she's in love with you. Or some idea of you." I wasn't about to cede her any legitimate territory. "Or some idea of love." I was sure my take on her was accurate, and I was sure Mac would agree. Once we started talking again, I figured we'd call a truce at the site of our common language, misplaced like a set of house keys for the last few hours, and

then I'd tell him what else I thought. "What did *you* think?"
I asked in the meantime.

"I was surprised and moved that she had such strong feelings
for me."

"Moved?"

"Of course. You could see she was having a hard time."

"Where exactly were you moved to?"

"Sorry?"

"I can appreciate you were surprised. But moved?"

"She spent all day looking for me, not finding me, thinking
she wouldn't. She was ragged by the time we saw her."

"It comes with the territory, Mac."

"What territory?"

"Did we just come from the same place?"

"What are you talking about?"

"She crashed a party she didn't even have the address for."

"Jesus, Kate, do we have to go through this again?"

"Again?"

"She saved us a trip to Paris. All right?"

For the better part of the next block, I said nothing and
Mac said nothing. We stared straight ahead or turned to look
out the windows of the beat-up Renault at this city we had
come to as a lark, a place to change planes, eat a few meals,
see the sights. We are unaccustomed to quarreling, and jealousy has never had a place in our differences.

"That was quite a display," I said finally, quietly, "and I
only understood the scenes with subtitles."

"I'm sure she'll be more relaxed tomorrow."

"If she isn't"—still quietly—"you'll have plenty of time to
calm her down. Eight or ten hours should do the trick."

He sighed, one of his deep, raspy sighs, a sigh you can hear
in the next room. It's what he does instead of yelling. "What

difference does it make how much time I spend with her?"

"Maybe for her next joint venture, Lida could beam Oprah to St. Petersburg. She could even be the star of the first show. 'Russian Women Who Love Too Much.' Just when you thought their only problems were breadlines and no queen-size pantyhose."

"What do you want from me?" Mac snapped.

"Have lunch with her and call it a day."

"I just made these plans. I can't very well cancel them now." Mac leaned forward and tapped the driver on his shoulder. "This is our hotel. Right here."

Mac handed him a bill, I crawled out and left the door open behind me. A moment later I heard it slam shut. Mac had closed it from inside. I felt my heart lurch. Was he going back to her hotel? I spun around.

He emerged from the other door and hoisted the camera to his shoulder. "You sure you don't want something to eat?"

I didn't know anymore who was speaking when words came out of his mouth, it was like a movie that had been dubbed: I heard English but didn't trust it. He sounded like himself now: even-tempered, solicitous. I shook my head.

"You want food or you don't?"

"Don't."

"What about a spin around the Grand'Place? I think it's just around the corner."

"Let's put the equipment upstairs."

"I'll do it." He started for the door of the hotel.

"I'll come with you."

I was afraid to let him out of my sight. We marched single file through the lobby and into the coffinlike elevator. Mac stood at my back. I pressed the "6" button until the lift began its slow, noisy ascent, calling attention to our silence, to everything we weren't saying. It was like the sounds of the bed creaking when you are making love with someone you don't know very well and you'd rather the metal springs weren't there to remind you. I was waiting for Mac to touch me, talk to me, place his hands on the seismograph and know just by touch the dimensions of my tremor. He is always so good at that. We crept from "3" to "4" to "5" in utter silence, the cold silence of a cell, and as the crate jerked to a stop on "6," I made my decision. I would leave a note for Eric under his door, with instructions. Eric—About t'mor: What I'd like you to do— But when I turned to glance at Mac stepping out of the elevator, my heart lurched again. A rivulet of tears trickled down one side of his face. The other cheek looked like it had just been wiped dry. He examined the key in his hand, not sure of our room number, and when he looked up and saw me staring, saw the fear in my eyes, he said something but so softly I couldn't hear it, and I was afraid to ask what it was because I was sure he would tell me, and I had had enough bad news for one night.

"I'm all right," he said quietly, and the door swung open. "I was just thinking that he would be twenty-two today."

As long as it's Sam he's longing for, I thought, and not Lida. Or maybe it wasn't just Sam. Maybe it was Lida who reminded him of Sam's childhood, of the years when Sam was alive. When Mac was whole. I followed him into our room and considered a darker possibility: that Mac was toying with me. He had wanted to silence me, to shield himself from my anger and knew his tears would do the trick. They had. They always did. I am a hostage to his grief. And when the subject is Sam, I never know what to say to him. I am as tongue-tied as everyone else. I needed to tell Mac how difficult this was for me, but every time I tried, he had shot back with how hard it was for him, or for Lida. And since I knew they had suffered over love in ways I never had, maybe what happened that night is that I became a hostage to their grief as well.

I unzipped my suitcase and pretended to search for something deep inside it, and perhaps that was what I was doing: looking for something I couldn't put my hands on. But what I came up with was a long flannel nightgown Mac had given me the first winter we were together. I had gone to Boston to raise money for a film, and a package arrived one morning at my hotel from a store I'd never heard of in San Francisco, this deep-blue flannel with little red dolphins around the collar. Keep Warm, Sparks, the card inside read, All My Love, S. I turned to him now, holding the nightgown up against me like I was measuring the fit. "Remember when you sent me this and I couldn't figure out who the hell 'S' was? I mean, I knew 'Sparks' was my name, but I didn't know it was yours yet."

He laughed a little. "Yeah."

I stepped forward and opened my arms to him, letting the nightgown fall between us, feeling the sleeves bunch up around my ankles, and Mac embraced me back, layers of leather and fabric in the way of our bare skin. We were comfortable, we fit, we held on tight, but there was more sorrow than passion to the way we clung, and I remembered an early morning in the kitchen of my childhood, my mother getting a phone call to say her brother had died. When she hung up, my father went to her and held her like this, the way Mac and I were holding each other, like mourners, not lovers. I saw them kiss on occasion, but that dark morning was the only time I ever saw them embrace. I reached my arm around Mac's neck and stroked the soft skin behind his ears. He did not pull away,

he let me rub and kiss his neck, but he did not touch me back
in kind.

"You ready?" he said softly.

"For what?"

"A walk around the Grand'Place." I shrank back and felt
the nightgown clump up between my feet like a pile of leaves.
"Should we bring a guidebook?"

He is usually so willing, and I am the one with work to do,
a deadline, an appointment I can't be late for. I bent over and
yanked the thing by a sleeve and tossed it onto the bed. Was
it really Sam he longed for? Was there someone he imagined
I wanted instead of him the times I turned him away? "I'm
not sure where the guidebook is," I said.

"We'll make do without it."

Our arms brushed as we left the room and I felt Mac grab
hold of my hand for a few seconds, a friendly, chin-up squeeze
you might give someone before she goes in for a root canal.
Buck up, pal. But we were nearly strangers again as we waited
for the elevator, and that was when I remembered the moment
in my friend's cabin three years before when I had said to
Mac, I'm afraid you'll dismiss my pain, whatever pain it is,
because it will never be as great as yours. He assured me that
competition of that sort was not in his nature. We stood at
the elevator without exchanging a word or a glance, as if we
were on our way not to the Grand'Place but to the doctor who
would measure the dimensions of our heads before sending
us into the Belgian Congo. I wasn't sure anymore what Mac's
nature was, or what my own was. The only one of us I thought
I had a clear fix on was Lida.

TEN

▼

A plate of croissants, triangles of Belgian butter, a bowl of raspberry jam, someone's shaggy terrier curled up like a snake on the banquette across the breakfast room of the Hôtel Petite Madeleine. Mac was leaving in ten minutes for Lida's hotel, and there was something I had to tell him.

"Are you going to eat your croissant?" he said.

"Yes."

"That pat of butter?"

"Take it."

The walls around us had been painted a deep cadmium red and the chairs and banquettes covered with a silky forest-green material. An odd choice of colors for this small, makeshift dining room, colors that made it seem cramped and cavernous and slightly louche. But they were familiar to me. I looked from surface to surface, cross-referencing this red and this green. And this silence between us. I heard every clink of coffee cup against saucer, the sound of Mac chewing, the dour concierge who had checked us in last night answering a guest's question: *No. No fax . . . Perhaps the Hilton.* For almost a month the sun does not set, her back arcs, her legs fall open, she circles his cock with her tongue. Or so I imagine, so I have come to believe.

"What will you and Lida do today?"

"We'll start at the Musées des Beaux-Arts, then I suppose—"

"The museums in Brussels are closed on Mondays."

"How do you know?"

"I told you last night. I read it in the guidebook. Don't you remember my saying so?"

"Where were we?"

"In our room."

"I don't remember. I guess we'll wander around."

I turned to the lace half-curtains, thickly textured fabric into which a swan design had been woven, that hung from a brass rod bisecting the window. "It's pouring out, Mac."

"We'll find a café."

"For seven hours?"

He glared at me as if I had insulted him, then leaned forward over his butter plate and spoke between clenched teeth. "If I wanted to screw her, I could do it in forty-five minutes." When I glared back, too startled to know what to say, he went on in anger but more quietly, because there were people sitting two tables away from us. "What the hell else do you want from me?" He had never spoken to me with such contempt. "Well?"

"I told you last night. Have lunch with her. Why do you have to spend seven—"

"Goddamnit, Kate, she's stranded here. Her friends have probably left for the day, I can't call her at this hour and— I'm due at her hotel in—"

"I forgot. Diplomats have to send engraved invitations a week before the event. Sorry to suggest such a breach of protocol."

"It has nothing to do with diplomacy."

"It certainly doesn't."

Then I heard Mac sigh, fill his lungs as if he were preparing to hunt for something on the bottom of a pool, and exhale so loudly the sound he made might be mistaken for a moan, and I knew this meant he was still angry and I was still not sure why. What I mean is that I was waiting for an overture, a concession, I'd have settled for a simple acknowledgment of how difficult he could surely see this was for me. He buttered the last of his croissant, and I knew he had never displayed such a willful disregard for what I wanted. I didn't know what else to say, I really didn't, and there were only a few minutes before he left. I had to tell him about Eric.

"I want you to know," I began, but stopped in midsentence. My plan had seemed such a good idea at two o'clock that morning as I remembered his time in Leningrad, and invented memories built on the stories he had told me during that long night in his bed three years before, when he did her lines in Russian and then in instantaneous translations, doing her in the original for no reason other than that the sound of it, the memory of the sound of it, the way she had said, *Nelzya, Mac, nelzya*, thrilled him. I loved it. I loved that he had wanted a woman as quick and rangy as Lida, as sure of herself as I often am of myself.

"You want me to know what?" he said now.

"Eric is going with you. He'll be down in a few minutes."

"To chaperon?"

"To shoot."

"Jesus, Kate. If you don't trust me, say so, but don't send someone to tail me."

"Of course I trust you," I said, and I think I was telling the truth. "This has nothing to do with trust. It has to do with *glasnost*." I could see Mac smile as I reached down into my bag. "Here's the cassette recorder." I handed it across the table. "And two sixty-minute tapes. It's more audio than Eric will have film stock, but we can work with that. Don't forget to slate it for sync. Turn it off whenever you like—I don't want you to feel that the place is bugged—but pay attention to when the camera's running, so I don't get more picture without sound. Make sure you've got it turned on for the most dramatic moments, like when the KGB shows up and the State Department freaks out. When should I expect you? Never mind, why don't we meet at the airport an hour before our flight leaves."

He said nothing for a moment, a long moment, startled by my transformation. It had surprised me too. "How much stock are you going through? And what's this movie about? Last night it was—"

"It's good material, Mac. I'm not sure what I'll do with it yet."

"Sparks, I went along with this last night because you wanted me to. But it doesn't seem fair to her today, I mean—"

"She didn't mind the camera."

He couldn't argue with that.

"And from what I saw, neither did you."

"It's an expensive home movie."

"So ask her where to buy an umbrella in Siberia and I'll sell the clip to the home-shopping channel."

"You're determined to do this?"

I nodded. I was. The more determined he was to see her, the more I was to get it on film.

"Okay. But I'd rather we go to the airport together. Why don't you meet us later?"

"I might go to Bruges, since all the museums here are closed. There's a Van Eyck I'd like to see. And maybe I'll run into Lida's friends." But I knew I wasn't going anywhere, except upstairs, back to our room. I hadn't slept more than a few hours all night. "If I don't go, we can get together."

"We should leave for the airport at five. Pick a time to meet us."

"Four-thirty. The Grand'Place, in front of the Town Hall."

"Thanks, Sparks."

"For what?"

"Giving Lida and me so much time together."

That had nothing to do with it. I just wanted to be spared the spectacle of their ardor.

Then we went back to our coffee and silence. I expected Mac to get up and leave any second and feared that if Eric was not down here, Mac would go without him. I looked from my empty plate to the deep red wall that framed Mac's face, to the chairs upholstered in that familiar green, until I realized where I had seen these colors before. They were the red and green that dominate Van Eyck's *Arnolfini Wedding.* I had a postcard of that painting above my desk for ten years, a souvenir of my first visit to the National Gallery in London. The week after I married Mac, I sent it to B.J. in an envelope, with a message on the back: "Marriage isn't as bad as everyone always says it is," and that was my last dispatch.

"Just act natural." Eric was giving orders from the doorjamb, the camera slung on his shoulder, emitting the comforting purr that told me it was rolling. "How much will you give me for the pickled body of Vladimir Ilyich Lenin, kept moist for sixty-seven years with the help of a mysterious embalming fluid and a team of molecular biologists? Do I hear a million rubles? Do I hear Michael Ovitz putting together a package? Danny DeVito is Lenin *before*, Roseanne Barr plays him once he's dead, and Public Enemy does the sound track?"

There is a six-second piece of footage of the two of us in that breakfast room turning to the camera, surprise dissolving into laughter, a few soothing seconds of comic relief. I remember how good it felt to laugh and hear Mac laugh too. I see it now on the screen. And I see myself turn away from the camera back to the breakfast table to look at Mac head-on. He was smiling, looking up at Eric, now over to me. I think he wanted to make sure I was still smiling, still capable of it, that there was some residual effect to Eric's endearing entrance. My back was to the camera, so I can't say exactly how I looked to Mac, but I remember feeling suddenly queasy about what was to come and wondering if I might feel different if I had managed to seduce him last night. My friend Nan used to say that one of the top three best things about sex is that you can be almost positive you have the other person's complete attention. Last night, his attention was all I had really wanted.

"Are we ready to roll?" Eric said.

"I'm ready when you are." Mac stood and leaned down and kissed me on the cheek. "Have a good time in Bruges. Don't miss the Memling."

I gave them my royal wave, held my forearm and hand straight up like a broomstick and rotated my wrist. Cute, but I could feel the fear gather in my stomach like the beginning of flu. "See you later, guys." I stood and watched them leave from the lace-curtained window, remembering the moment last night when Lida told us she had called her friend Susan in Chicago to report on the whereabouts of my husband. Later in the day I would call Nan in New York to report on the whereabouts of my husband. No matter who comes and who goes, the women are on the phone keeping score, keeping track, moving colored pushpins across a map of the world: your man was last seen right here—on the curb outside the Petite Madeleine, raising his arm to catch a cab.

Whatever Eric managed to shoot and Mac managed to pick up on the audio would be good material for something, someday. But the real reason I sent Eric along, the real reason I forced the tape deck on Mac was that I wanted to watch. I still couldn't take my eyes off the two of them. I wasn't really worried that Mac would sleep with her, not today. There was a better chance he would fall into something like love with her again, if he hadn't already.

ELEVEN

The trees are bare, the sky is the color of ash.

"This is not normal," says a strange woman's voice. The shot is wide, a city park with uniform trees, quadrangles of soggy grass, and a wooden bench painted green, on which Mac and Lida are sitting, their backs to the camera. You cannot see the cassette player that must be on Mac's lap. The voice isn't Lida's, but it's her words spoken in English by a woman who translated and dubbed them. On the other sound track, much softer, is Lida's own voice in Russian. "Last night I thought this movie business was a joke. Maybe not a joke. But it's not funny now. Not normal. Turn it off." Off it goes.

The back of the bench, the backs of their heads, picture without sound. I am about to fast-forward when I hear another voice. "Mac has just turned off the tape deck." Is that Eric? "At least it looks like that from here. I'm twenty feet away, leaning against a tree, trying to be inconspicuous." It is. "Svetlana blows hot and cold on the surveillance. Christ, it's starting to rain again. But Lida comes prepared. She whips out a black fold-up umbrella from her shoulder bag and pops it open." That's exactly what's happening on-screen. "Isn't there a Magritte painting of a man in a bowler hat holding up an open umbrella, and a bright blue sky above? If there isn't, there should be. I can't see an open umbrella in Brussels without thinking of that painting. Or what I think is that painting. I have no idea what Mac and Olga Baclanova are whispering about underneath theirs. You know who she is, don't you, Kate? The Russian actress who made it in Hollywood silent films and then starred in *Freaks* in the thirties, as the viper who married a circus freak for money? One of three stars who survived the transition to talkies, because she sounded like she came from Russia, not Brooklyn.

"I'm not very good at this, in case you haven't noticed in the ten years we've been doing business. Like I said in Brussels, I'm a coward. That is, when I'm not downright stroppy. I should have said yes when you wanted me to turn off the camera, and no to a few other things, but I had no idea what was going on behind the scenes. It's true I ended up spying on them, but that doesn't mean I could see the big picture. All I had was the view through the keyhole.

"In the cab that morning on our way to her hotel, Mac told me her husband is a big exec with Air France. Her knight in shining armor rides a 737-Stretch. I suppose you know that by now, or knew it all along. Sweetheart, have you considered this angle? Poor girl from Soviet Union marries well, escapes to West, thinks it's paradise from here on out, but learns that life among the bourgeoisie is as boring as it was with the Commies, except the lines aren't as long and the rubbers don't break. She gets nostalgic for all that deprivation and all that roiling Russian emotion. She's bored to tears in the suburbs doing the dutiful housewife number and fighting with the old man over who does the laundry while she exports Pampers to the Ukraine. So she fixates on happy days of yore with Mac. Let's call him: Best Male in a Limited Series. You won't read this in *The New York Review of Books* but Soviet men are lousy in bed. Why do you think everyone wants to leave? Did you know Soviet women actually believe American men are *gallant* because they say 'excuse me' and hold open doors? I know that wasn't all she wanted from Comrade MacKenzie, but give it a few minutes from her point of view. I refer you to a passage in the novel about Cold War Berlin you lent me that I haven't gotten around to returning. Schneider-the-author/narrator is talking about the feelings West Berliners had for their brethren in the East, before the Wall came down: 'In their separation pangs they resemble a lover grieving not so much for his loved one as for the strong emotion he once felt.' Jesus, Kate, she was twenty-three, and Mac had a hell of a lot more going for him than the pimply Swiss boyfriend who brought her Levi's and a few bootlegged Stevie Wonder albums. So what it was only three weeks? So much the better. She never had a chance to find out how tedious love can be once the fireworks fizzle. Come to think of it, I've never stuck around for the boring bits either. The rain's picking up, sweetheart. Looks like they're moving camp. Stay dry. And forgive me."

Eric doctored the sound track. He must have recorded this as soon as we got back from Turkey five days ago, sat at someone's Steenbeck with a tape recorder and spouted. And then left instructions for the lab to lay the sound next to this picture.

He saw nearly all of what there was to see in Brussels but barely let on—until he was right up against it—that he'd been paying attention. He is different from Mac that way. When

the going gets tough, Mac crosses his fingers and hopes everything will turn out fine, despite all the evidence to the contrary.
Eric is more interested in the journey than the arrival. He goes
along for all sorts of rides, just to see where they might lead.
He doesn't dwell on outcomes one way or the other, maybe
because he hasn't lost as much as Mac has. Or maybe because
he never wanted as much to begin with. And different from
Mac in other ways too. I don't just mean that Mac will stick
around for the boring parts and the wife who works on New
Year's Eve, I mean that Mac is ordinarily attentive in a way
you hear women complain that their men are not. A married
woman I admire once told me that she had had three children
because she was so lonely. "Your marriage doesn't help that?"
Her husband is a kind, devoted, but very busy man. She shook
her head sadly at my question. It was before I knew Mac, and
I think she meant, in that shake of her head, to caution me,
to warn me about what to expect from love.

On the Steenbeck screen in front of me, there's a long shot
of Mac and Lida in her trenchcoat walking off into the rain,
under her umbrella. She is holding my husband's arm. It's a
small umbrella. There is no stunning blue sky up above.

Cut to the two of them walking down a narrow, busy sidewalk with what look like Christmas lights strung up in the
distance, straddling a street of beautiful old row houses. They
stop at the window of a shop, look in, keep moving. Eric
lingers on the window, an arty display of comic books, the
covers immensely bold and bright, more like posters than
comics.

Another sidewalk, a busy block of narrow townhouses. Lida
swerves right and points to a plaque on a door. Close-up of
brass plaque: Musée Horta. Close-ups of art nouveau details

of façade, M. Horta's house, his beautiful oak door, loopy lead-glass design on the top half, the brass handle, delicate as a twig. Mac reaches to pull it. It's locked. He moves closer to read the plaque. *Fermé les lundis.* They turn and shrug theatrically for Eric. Lida crosses her magnificent eyes and laughs at her antics. It's Monday in Brussels.

This footage might as well be outtakes for an American Express commercial, a prosperous middle-aged couple in a prosperous foreign city, trying to look as if they are having a good time. Maybe they are. I see only their backs, their profiles, their most public selves, Lida extending her hand past the edge of the umbrella to feel for rain.

They enter a posh pâtisserie called the Café d'Or. There's a marzipan Christmas tree in the window, and tables and chairs against a far wall. Eric shoots them from outside, through the wide glass, the soft-pink neon sign that says, in lovely, upright neon script, SPECIALITÉS AU GRAND MARNIER. The cassette recorder sits between them on the table. They will order espresso, perhaps a slice of the glazed strawberry tart displayed in the window. Eric zooms in tight. Lida listens and Mac talks, not a sentence here and a sentence there but a full-blown tale. The tape recorder is still off but I imagine him telling her the story of the investigation.

He'd been back from Leningrad for almost three months when he got a phone call one morning in his office. His secretary announced there was a Susan Pollet on the line, "and she says you know her."

"Susan, how've you been?"

"Positively groovy, until your two buddies showed up. They got here an hour ago and I just managed to pry them from the door."

"I don't know what you're talking about. Where are you?"

"New York. My parents' place. Didn't you give them this
address?"

"Give who?"

"They flashed some State Department IDs in my face. Said
they were with security and they wanted to ask me some questions about you. Why didn't you warn me?"

"This is the first I've heard of any of this. What did they
want to know?"

"About you and Lida. The hard-core. I said I didn't know
anything. Nada. Then I tried to nudge them out the door.
Then they told me that I had delivered a letter from you to
Lida six weeks ago when I went back there to visit. How the
hell did they know that? Are you going to tell me I'm under
surveillance for bringing a letter to a friend? The U.S. government doesn't have anything better to do than—"

"Susan, I don't know what's going on, I'm in the dark on
this right now." Then it occurred to him that his phone calls
were being monitored, not only by the KGB, which everyone
figured anyway, but by the State Department too.

"They also wanted to know if you and I were quote sexually
intimate unquote. I told them, not on your life."

"If they come back, tell them the truth about Lida and me."

"Are you crazy?"

"This wasn't a secret, I made sure it wasn't. I took her to
that cocktail party at the consul general's where I introduced
you to her. Remember? Why they're after me all of a
sudden—"

"Someone must have ratted on you."

Mac was silent, backpedaling through a maze of distant
names and faces, wives, nannies, maids, the skinny wife of
the deputy station chief who had lectured him once on Peter
the Great's sarcophagus at the Hermitage. Had she been at

the consul general's cocktail party too? He could not remember. It could have been one of the men he worked with, but why wait to turn him in this way, three months after the fact?

"I suppose you're just getting what you deserve," Susan said. "Lida lost two jobs because of you. It's only fair that you should lose one." Mac knew that Susan had had it in for him since he had introduced her to Lida: the slick diplomat who cheats on his wife. Or maybe Susan had wanted Mac to cheat with *her*.

"You told me she got another job," he said. Lida had not written any of this in her letters, she knew it wasn't safe.

"You can probably get another one too, Mac. Good bullshitters can always get work in Washington."

Her nastiness stung like a pinprick, a short, sharp pain, and then it was gone. "I'm sorry you had to be involved in this. If they come back, tell them the truth." When he hung up, he dialed the number for the State Department security office. He wanted to exonerate himself, to make sure they understood he had nothing to hide. He would offer to come in right away and give a statement. He would tell them he had asked for a security briefing the morning he arrived in Leningrad and had been turned away flatly, told there wasn't a secure room in the building. If he had broken the rules, well, he had never been told what they were. "I understand you're conducting an investigation of me," he said to the receptionist who answered the phone.

"Would that be in the category of a background routine periodic checkup?"

He almost laughed. "I don't think so."

He insisted to the end that he had done nothing wrong, that he had asked for the briefing, that Gary Tucker hadn't thought it worth giving him, that he conducted himself, with

Lida and everyone else he encountered, in a manner befitting his position. His first and only loyalty was to his country, and had he ever been forced to choose between duty and desire— he would have given her up in an instant. And had he known, had he been told he must never invite a Soviet citizen into his flat, much less his bed, he would have complied. He would have eaten his dinner at RESTAURANT 25 and gone home alone, as he had every night until that one.

He insisted on all of this in meeting after meeting, in no- tarized affidavits, confidential memoranda. The State De- partment finally conceded that Gary Tucker had erred in not providing a briefing—they tracked him down in Lebanon to confirm the story—but they did not concede the larger point, that any Foreign Service officer assigned to the Soviet Union "is expected to have the judgment not to place himself in a position where Soviet Intelligence could exploit him, bring pressure on him, or use his actions to bring discredit upon the United States," according to the letter of reprimand that sat in his personnel file for five years. "Your conduct and unre- ported contacts with this Soviet woman have put you in such a position. A prudent officer of your background and experi- ence at a post as sensitive and hostile as Leningrad should not have done what you did."

I keep thinking there should be an immutable right answer, an up-or-down vote on the correctness of Mac's conduct in Leningrad. If I were voting, which way would I lean? Probably toward Mac, a vote for adventure, for romance, for the sound- ness of his judgment. On the other hand, I see their point. He should have proceeded with more caution. If he had been a properly ambitious Foreign Service officer, on the straight- and-narrow career path, his eye firmly on the Seventh Floor, he would have. And if Lida had not been quite so irresistible,

and his marriage so close to tatters, he might have. Brussels
is another story, but I am still looking for the one right answer,
an up-or-down vote on who is to blame for what happened.
Lida is the prime suspect, but she was not acting alone, she
had plenty of help from us. She said jump and we jumped,
she said listen and we listened, she said pay attention and we
did. But who were we when we handed over the reins to her,
and to whom might we relinquish them next time?

▼

TWELVE

Great faces on Mac's list. Sophia Loren. Jeanne Moreau. A girl in a Fantin-Latour portrait he saw once at the Jeu de Paume. A Malaysian woman who came to the consulate in Kuala Lumpur in 1966, so shy that she barely raised her almond-shaped eyes from the desk that separated them. Mac approved her visa, then snitched one of the postage-stamp-size photos she had to submit with the application and still has it in a carton of mementos. And Lida. He glances at her profile before the lights go down at the Kirov. Her cheekbones are chiseled, her complexion roseate, as if she has just come in his arms. They are careful in public not to touch. Except like this: thigh to thigh in their theater seats.

Her eyes wander over the marvelous stage curtain, a dense antique confection of sky-blue silk and brocade and shiny tassels, breathtakingly opulent, as three KGB agents monitor every move from the balcony. The lights go down and the curtain opens on a single performer, a man in a white leotard and tights, curled up in the center of the stage, as compact as a human form can make itself. He raises his head and opens his limbs in gestures no larger than millimeters, not much faster than the petals of a tulip opening in sunlight. Mac and Lida stare in awe, as if what they're witnessing is a man teetering on a hundredth-story ledge instead of sitting cross-legged on a floor, moving as slowly as he can. The exquisite drama of near stasis. The dance is called *The Creation of the World*. The dancer is Baryshnikov. The beauty of it takes Mac's breath away.

The next afternoon in Mac's car, on their way back from the palace at Pavlovsk, she wants to learn to drive. "Teach me," she says. "The road is deserted."

They switch seats and he begins to explain the gears, the stick shift. The road is rutted and narrow and there is no white line. She starts the ignition immediately and stalls. He goes through it again, demonstrating with his hands the pedal motion of her foot letting up on the clutch and easing down on the accelerator. She watches, nods, turns the key with enormous concentration. The car takes off like a rocket going sideways. Lida's terror evaporates into dumb thrill, as if she were a kid on a roller coaster. Mac points. A large van appears on the road, it's come from a hidden driveway and seems to be heading straight for them. She panics and makes a sharp right turn off the road. The car barrels down a steep bank toward a spinney of pine trees. Mac is shouting, "Brake! Brake!" They shimmy to a standstill inches from a waist-high stump. Mac bangs open his door and looks down. He covers his eyes with his hand. Mud. Lida is laughing hysterically.

They are expected in two hours for cocktails at the consul general's residence, where Mac plans to introduce her to his colleagues, so the KGB won't be able to blackmail him.

"Don't worry," she tells him. "I'll go up to the road and find someone to pull us out. A farmer with a tractor. Whose car is this anyway?"

"It belongs to the consulate." Mac is someone who takes charge in emergencies, animated by problems that need solving, machines that must be brought to the scene, but for a few moments he feels a crushing inertia. They will never get out of here. The car will sink. It will cost him a fortune. And how will he explain himself?

"Mac, what's wrong? You don't like my driving? Two or three more lessons, I'll be ready to drive a bus."

The walls and glass cabinets of the consul general's mansion are filled with sterling candlesticks, antique sconces, Indian candelabra, Persian camel bags, African masks, evidence of a lifetime of foreign travel, exotic posts, of U.S. dollars in Third World countries. Mac, in a three-piece summer suit, introduces Lida to the host and hostess. "Thank you for lovely invitation," Lida says. The consul general is an old Soviet hand, can take you through the history and workings of the Politburo with the precision of an entomologist at a podium. His staff meetings are interminable, legendary. The Sovs are at it again, he'll begin. Now they tell us we can't import more than four cases per household per quarter, including the Fourth of July allotment, and that's down from eight cases last year at this time. I think they're using salami tactics on us. I hear that the Sovs have it in for Stockmann's. Has anyone had problems with shipments from Helsinki? Anyone heard that Stockmann's has gotten crosswise with the Sovs? Frankly, Emily and I have no complaints, but when we were in Havana, we swore by Ostermann's of Copenhagen, and we're prepared to buck the tide and go back to them if the Sovs are determined to make us jump through so many damn hoops to buy a case of Scotch.

But tonight, upon meeting Lida, all he says is "So nice to see you," a Washington welcome, a greeting that covers all bases, designed for men who've shaken so many hands that they don't know anymore whom they've already met.

"Thanks for having us," Mac says.

"Our pleasure. Mac, you know our nanny, Susan Pollet, don't you?"

"Susan. Of course."

The three of them drift away from the receiving line, Mac, Lida, and Susan, and cluster by the table of hors d'oeuvres making small talk in Russian. Mac keeps one eye on the rest of the crowd. He needs to introduce Lida to a few more of them. Gary Tucker, the deputy consul general; Bill Lank, the CIA communicator; Tom Ravenel, the admin officer. Needs to introduce her formally, so no one can accuse him of keeping her a secret. "Tom," he'll say, "I'd like you to meet a friend of mine, Lida Podryadchikova." Mac reaches for her elbow. "There's someone I'd like you to meet," he whispers, "one of the men I work with. He's a nice guy. You'll like him."

"As much as I like you?"

"I hope not."

"Who's that woman with the big nose speaking Russian by the bar?"

"I think she's with Gosplan."

Lida brushes elbows with her on her way to the bathroom. Even the consul general's house is swarming with informers.

In the center of the single ring, two clowns do a routine with a paper cup and an inflatable beach ball tied to a long string. One places the cup on his bald head, the other, from ten feet away, tries to knock it off with the beachball-on-a-string. The ball hits him everywhere but the head, and the paper cup remains, as if glued, on his shiny pate. Then they turn to the audience, point to a man sitting in the front row, gesture for him to join them. Lida laughs and claps, urging him on. But Mac needs no encouragement, you would think he was a shill, a member of the company. He leaps up and into the ring. He sees children everywhere, up and down the aisles, clear into the rafters. If only his kids— Where are they? What time is it in Washington? He is so disoriented, with the nights lasting as long as they do, sundown near midnight, love around the clock. He will have to tell them he saw the Leningrad circus, that the clowns picked him to stand in the center of the ring. If they could see him now, being thwacked on the head, the beachball bouncing off his chest, hundreds of children laughing, clowns with feet the shape of whales, their noses the color of fire, they would forgive him; he is certain they would forgive him all his errors, his absences, the uneven love he bears their mother, the lie he will tell them about the circus. I went with a friend who works at the consulate. Pow! The paper cup tumbles to the ground. Again! Mac cries. Try again! he begs them. But he hears too much feeling in his voice for this, a paper cup, a one-ring circus. He must be pleading with his wife, talking to himself.

In Peter the Great's Summer Garden Mac watches an old man clean a marble statue of Helios, sponging clean the thighs and patting them dry with cotton balls. The garden's walkways, along the left bank of the Neva, are lined with life-size Italian statuary displayed on tall pedestals. Peter the Great had wanted his gardens to rival Versailles. There would be fountains, magnificent trees, statues of gods and heroes. Everything but the fountains is still there. Mac takes a picture of the old man, touched by his tenderness with the marble, cleaning the toes as if this is his lover, his child, his life's work. He will call Lida over to watch, but when he turns to look for her, she is gone. He wanders to the adjacent walkway, then to the next, but he is looking in the wrong place. She is aloft. She meets his gaze over the shoulder of the tall white statue she embraces, clings to, perched on a few inches of pedestal. She's hip to hip with a Greek warrior, both hands on his buttocks, one leg wrapped around the backs of his knees.

"Take a picture!" she cries. She smiles for Mac's camera but he does not move. "Hey, what's wrong?" Can she detect his startled gaze from so far away? The image, the proportions, are so vivid, so exact, he forgets for a moment that she is humping a piece of stone. "Don't tell me you're jealous!"

"Of course not."

"So hurry up with the picture," she calls out. "He's about to come!"

Late the following afternoon, a three-line telex is carried into Mac's office and placed on his desk. He is waiting for information from Washington about the visa of a Soviet woman who has just gotten permission to visit her dying grandmother in Baltimore, but this telex—it takes no more than the first four words to guess the rest of them—is not the one he had been expecting.

"Take a right at the end of this block."

"Where are we going?"

"And a left at the bridge. On the other side, go right after the statue of Lenin, then straight for two kilometers. How was your day at work, my love?"

Lida had never asked about his work, and Mac did not often volunteer. She must have something to tell him. Just as he had something to tell her. "Uneventful," he lied. "How was yours?"

"Normal. First thing in the morning, before I went in, your nanny friend Susan called me. I told her about our arrangements tomorrow for *Boris Godunov*, I said we would pick her up at seven. Did I tell you my friend Katya is having a baby? Well, her mother-in-law is driving her to the brink. She stays in bed all day and sends Katya out to buy hair coloring and lipstick." She had never mentioned a Katya to him; he knew the name only from overhearing her conversation with Stazi. In fact, all of this sounded rather like her conversation with Stazi: significant for all she was not saying. "Take a right up here. Follow that truck. Then I talked to Volodya, a real character, a friend from high school. The first person I went to bed with. I *know* I told you about him."

"Of course," he lied. The KGB must have approached her. Or contacted her boss. Ordered the boss to give her an ultimatum: Tell us what you know about the American or you're out of a job. In his rearview mirror was the beige Lada that followed him everywhere. Mac smiled. Where had the bastards been when Lida drove the car off the road into a swamp? They might have radioed to headquarters for a tractor.

"His parents had a dacha outside Pushkin and we used to sneak out there and screw when we were supposed to be at these deadly all-day Komsomol meetings, before they had the good sense to kick me out. They kicked both of us out, but by that time, we were sick of each other. Look how gray the sky is. With such soupy thick clouds, we can forget the White Nights tonight. He called this morning to say he's having problems with his girlfriend. He wanted my advice. I said, Look, Volodya, when it comes to screwing women, I don't have much experience. It doesn't count, playing doctor with your sister when we were eleven . . ."

The tsars' old city was behind them and here was the Soviet Union. Narrow, desolate roads, paved as if the workmen had quit in the middle of the job. Immense fields of bright green weeds, and in the middle of them, like tents pitched in the wilderness, dismal high-rise apartment buildings. No paths, no shops, no landscaping, just tall gray boxes hundreds of yards from the road, clotheslines strung across all the terraces, sheets and wet socks dripping from end to end. No driveways, no parking lots, no cars. Except that one abandoned over there. The windshield smashed, the tires gone. Where on earth was she taking him? What could it be that she had to tell him? Was she pregnant? But she could tell him that anywhere. And how would she know so soon? They had only known each other for two weeks and four days.

"You can park just beyond those pillars."

It looked like some sort of park from up here, this raised stone terrace leading down a wide flight of steps to vast manicured lawns surrounded by a great circle of evergreens. He caught only a phrase or two engraved on the side of a pillar: "Valorous defenders . . . the lives of the fallen."

"I told you I would take you sometime to Piskarev. This is it." She was matter-of-fact, distant, the perfect Intourist guide, leading him down the steps past a flame burning in the center of an iron grate—"that's the eternal flame"—and down more steps to the wide formal walkway lined with flower beds and flanked on both sides by raised strips of lawn that lay perpendicular to the walkway, rows and rows like a bowling alley with narrow gravel paths between grassy mounds and a low, stout headstone at each end.

"At first, people were buried normally in cemeteries. But after February of '42, they were all brought here. No one had the strength to dig the frozen ground, so the local air defense groups dynamited it, blasted the huge pits we are walking over. In the late fifties, they decided to turn it into a memorial. They added these granite headstones." Mac saw only "1942" chiseled onto all of them; stray flowers lay like pickup sticks on their flat tops. "They added the sidewalks, the trees, and of course the statue of the Motherland you see at the end of the walkway. She is six meters high, made of bronze. That snakelike thing she holds is a garland of oak and laurel leaves which she will place on the graves of the nameless heroes. This place opened in 1960. Officially there are 800,000 people here. Almost all died of starvation. Let's keep walking. Unofficially, one and a half million. Stalin wanted to keep the numbers lower, so that Leningrad didn't acquire the distinction of a tortured city. He despised Leningrad. If Stalin had had his way— Oh, Mac—"

He is as emotional as they are, all these Russians who come to mourn a member of the family and find themselves stripped bare, weeping for everyone they have ever known, the living and the dead, his children and his parents. She kissed the half-dozen tears from his face and he remembered the shock of leaning into his father's casket to kiss him goodbye and hitting his front tooth on a cheek that had turned to porcelain.

"I'm all right."

"Of course."

He reached for her hands. "I have something to tell you. I got a telex today from Washington."

Her hands were warm, they were the size of his, and at the end of his introduction, he heard her take a sharp, shallow breath. "Your wife?"

"My government."

She nodded. She knew at once. "When?"

"In four days."

She started to smile nervously, the way you do sometimes at bad news, because there is no facial expression reserved exclusively for sorrow. "Well." This time her breath was deeper, a sigh, as if she was in need of oxygen. "Let's keep walking It's best for us to stay away from the periphery." The tour was continuing, and she was still in charge, though she had just been told of a slight change in the itinerary. "Away from the gardens and trees. And our pals who've taken up positions at the hem of the skirt of the Motherland. My husband called me today."

"Who?"

"My Jewish friend. The guy from Siberia."

"Is he all right?"

"He's excellent. He just got permission to leave, to go to Israel. He applied years ago."

"Does he need a divorce?"

"To the contrary, he wants to return the favor I did for him. He invited me to go with him. Come, this way. We'll pay our respects to my grandmother. He said it would be quite easy for me, you know, since we're married."

"What is that?"

"What?"

"That music."

"It sounds like Chervinsky."

"Where's it coming from?"

"There are loudspeakers attached to those trees. See them? Little boxes. The sound is somewhat distorted."

"It's funeral music."

"Chervinsky's 'Funeral Melodies for Chorus and Orchestra.' "

"Does it play all the time?"

"There's a variety, so you don't grow tired of it if you come here often. Like those women." Lida tipped her chin toward a group of five gray-faced *babushkas* loping down the path with their bouquets of gladioli.

"You'll go with him, won't you?"

"To Israel? It isn't my idea of—"

"You don't have to end up there. First you go to Vienna to be processed. Then you can go wherever you want. And if it's just a favor, if it's nothing personal the way it was with Heinrich, then you're free to go where you please."

They turned down a gravel path, walking between two raised mounds of grass, and Mac wondered how deep the bodies went if there were almost a million beneath them.

"Free. And all alone."

"But not for long."

"No?"

"Of course not."

She stopped and turned to him, she was starting to smile. "Do you mean that?"

But he did not know what he meant, what he wanted, what he could offer her. A married man just passing through. If he could bear to leave his wife, if he could bear to leave his children, he knew he would have to leave his job too. "With those eyes of yours, you'll be wildly popular in major cities around the world."

He reached for her hands, but her eyes dimmed, her countenance shifted to neutral, and the expression was so unfamiliar, so unlike her, that to Mac she looked forlorn.
"I think it's starting to rain," she said. She wanted to change the subject, to steer them away from Mac's leaving Leningrad and her staying. "I think I felt a drop."

He wanted to comfort her, to encourage her, but what could he say? Jump, and maybe I will work up the nerve to catch you? To leave my wife and kids. To quit my job, because they would never let me marry you and keep my security clearance, even if you gave up your citizenship and joined the Junior League of Georgetown. Jump? And call me from London or New York—call me from Tel Aviv—and then maybe I will jump myself? It was not much of an offer: indecision, self-doubt, unemployment.

"I can tell you don't believe me," she said.

"About what?" Had she read all this on his face?

"The rain. The clouds look nasty. Let's get out of here."

Mac reached to touch her cheek, but she turned away just then, hurried down the walkway, pressing her shoulder bag hard against her hip. Mac understood her departure had nothing to do with the weather. She was embarrassed she had taken him all the way out here just to be told he didn't want her after all.

What do I know and what do I invent?

I imagine embraces, acts of love, pillow talk, some of the dirty bits. Here and there I see myself in the way she enjoys her pleasure. But the rest—I see Russia entirely through Mac's lens, his hazy, romantic filter, his empathy for the dispossessed, his contempt for the pompous bureaucrats in the consulate. All of it comes to me as in a dream in which you speak a language you don't know, find your way, somehow, around a country you have never been to. I have only ever seen pictures of Piskarev, a sixty-five-acre spectacle of love and death and longing. It does not matter that there are no names engraved in black granite, in an alphabet I know how to read, and that in photographs you might think it is an ordinary park. It is the place I know best of all.

Did it really threaten to rain that evening, or was there another evening of rain I confused with this one? I don't know, but it suits me here: rain as a device to wrap up a scene that offers no clear-cut ending. I don't have a transcript of what Lida said or Mac said, and maybe he didn't cry after all. But Mac did tell me that after that night, they never spoke again about her leaving Leningrad or about their future. Even in the letters they wrote back and forth once he returned to the States, they did not imagine meetings, they ventured nothing more than the vague yearnings of separated lovers. She wrote, for instance: "Here is the photograph you sent me of yourself. It's a Russian superstition that if you exchange pictures, you will never see each other again." It could be I'm the one who cried at Piskarev. I'm the one who can't bear to see him go.

In Brussels, I sat on the bed of our hotel room two blocks from the Grand'Place, trying to read the *International Herald Tribune*. I had to read certain sentences two and three times to make sense of them, and when I succeeded, I realized I hadn't cared what was said to begin with. When the phone rang at the stroke of noon, I was sure it was Mac.

▼

THIRTEEN

"Up for a movie?"

"What?"

"The new Rohmer is showing at one."

"Mac?"

"Eric."

"Where's Mac?"

"They told me to get lost. Actually, I had no choice. They were sitting around this *pâtisserie* for two hours. I came and went, got a few minutes of footage. Then they split and got a cab."

"Where to?"

"No idea."

"How long ago?"

"Ten minutes. Look, this flick starts in an hour, the theater's right around the corner from our hotel in the Galeries St.-Hubert. Let's grab a bite and then do it."

It had been foolish to think they would tote Eric around all day like a Baedeker, but hearing that they were on their own gave me a fright, the sensation of your foot slipping at the edge of a stair before you can grab the banister.

"Kate, are you there?"

"Yeah. I'm looking over my production schedule for Turkey, and I've got to make a few phone calls. Let's stick to four-thirty, the Grand'Place." I let the receiver drop into the cradle and stared at the phone, tried to memorize its shape, its stillness, the ten finger holes, the distance between here and there, wherever they had taken their taxi to. Nothing incriminating about getting into a taxi. They might have been in one earlier, taken one to the *pâtisserie*. When it's raining, it's not uncommon for people to take taxis. I kept staring at the telephone and talking things over with myself. I picked up the receiver to phone Nan in New York, but as I put it to my ear, I knew I had already made up my mind. Call it checking the burners on the stove before you go to sleep at night, trekking back from the waiting elevator to make sure you've double-locked the door. I grabbed my shoulder bag, lumbered down six flights of stairs, and found a taxi of my own.

"Le Saint-Simon."

I had not yet seen the city in daylight, or the melancholy pallor that passes for it most days of the year. Men in their Burberry trenchcoats and black umbrellas with fine wood handles. The Episcopalian stylishness of the women. Republican cloth coats, the camel's hair, the tweed, the only brushstrokes of bright color hot pink or magenta, in a scarf or umbrella. A chic young woman stopped on a street corner to consult her Filofax for the address of her next appointment. They all looked as if they were on their way to the Church of the Heavenly Rest on upper Fifth Avenue, which Nan always calls the Church of the Very Well Dressed. Volvos and Mercedeses lined the curbs with their diplomatic plates and windshield wipers that never rest, well-groomed lap dogs pulled every leash and squatted in the rain, their plastic plaid raincoats buckled around their miniature middles. I was taking an inventory of everything I could name, buses, shop signs, license plates, iron gates, mansard roofs, and a man bearing a double umbrella—one handle supporting two cloth covers, attached like Siamese twins—something I'd seen advertised in an airline magazine. When I turned and saw my face in the rearview mirror, my likeness startled me. I think I had been expecting a young Englishwoman with too much makeup and a felt cloche, Jean Rhys as a character in one of her novels, diminished, near panic, taking a taxi she can't afford to a place she isn't welcome. Why do you suppose, I once asked Mac, Lida chose the cemetery to tell you about her invitation to Israel? Privacy, he said, no informers among the dead, and regardless of what happened between us, she didn't want to ruin her friend's chance to leave. But now I knew there was more: she was given to theatrical gestures, and what better place than Piskarev to soften the resolve, tug at the heartstrings of a man like Mac. And showing up in Brussels this way, three weeks early in the wrong country—she wanted to catch us off guard. She had come to try again, with her pocketful of Kleenex and her cellular phone. The sight of a woman crying, a woman he had loved in need—Mac was as soft as butter.

We crossed a wide boulevard lined with skyscrapers, glass buildings topped with lighted monikers, IBM, XEROX, SABENA, HYATT. I wanted to be farther away, in a city as exotic as Brussels had seemed last night when we came upon the luminescent plaza outside our hotel, as unfamiliar as Leningrad had seemed in my reveries all morning. It is what you want from travel, to be altered, transported, swept into another world. But here is what it comes down to: IBM, XEROX, HYATT, the numbing banality of your husband off with another woman. And this: bitter reminders of another trip to Europe that ended badly, my mother and I on a wide-eyed grand tour when I was sixteen, a first for both of us. Every street corner, every merchant's window, every coin was an event, a Byronic adventure, another brilliant facet of the globe we barely knew. When we got home, their marriage spiraled into months of guerrilla warfare. As my brother, my sister, and I left the apartment for school in the morning, we would pass my father returning home to change his shirt. Or maybe he was there at that hour only to let us know he had not come home that night. It was the late 1960s, and I think my father had spent his life waiting for the times to catch up to him. When I was thirteen or fourteen, in the living room where he used to sit with his binoculars, he told me about a girl he had known in college. "I thought I had the greatest deal on the campus, so I didn't tell anyone else how much she loved to screw." I am a good listener, and I remember everything, this anecdote and a dozen others he recited to me like history lessons. "A few months later, I find out she's banging everyone else in my frat house. Women like that—they're called nymphomaniacs." The living room, the most treacherous country of all.

"*Madame*," said the cabdriver, "*nous sommes ici.*"

"Please ring Lida Martelle's room."

"One moment." The young man at the desk was lithe, epicene in the way of dancers and certain European men. His steps were small, his movements excessively careful. He slipped a set of headphones over his ears, ran his forefinger down a sheet of paper searching for her name. I hadn't come to find them here, but to find them gone. Absent. No sign whatsoever. As soon as he rang her room and said there was no answer, I'd split and not tell Mac I had come. The young man punched three buttons I couldn't see on a key pad. I noticed I was holding my breath. Of course they're not here. Mac's belligerence, his obstinacy last night and this morning—I couldn't explain them, but the moment we left for Istanbul all of this would shrink to its proper size: a bout of Cold War nostalgia, a twenty-four-hour stopover with a special bonus coupon not for the faint at heart.

"No one answers," the clerk said.

"Is she in her room?"

He turned and checked the open mail slots behind him. "The key is here." He pushed a notepad toward me. "Do you want to write a message?"

Nothing that would fit on a piece of paper so small. I shook my head. "Is there somewhere I can get a cup of coffee?"

"The bar."

"Thank you."

I crossed the crowded threshold half expecting to see them there, and maybe that was why I went in, to check the faces in the mirror against the back wall and the couples in the booths. The place was packed with Belgians and German businessmen on their lunch hour. I stepped up to a barstool and ordered an espresso. I had read in a guidebook that there are fifteen hundred restaurants in Brussels, but here I was, here I might very well stay for the rest of the afternoon. They would show up sooner or later, I was sure of it. And Mac would be so surprised to see me here, more surprised than he had been to find Lida in Brussels. I have never been shy about looking for men in places where they don't belong. One night when I was five and my mother was putting me to sleep, I asked her where Daddy was. "In the city." "But where?" "I'm not sure."

"Try '21,' " I told her. "And if he's not there, call Coco Tucker." She might have gotten around to these calls on her own, but my instructing her with such blasé certainty, such innocent goodwill—and the fact that that night, she found him at "21"—became a story my father liked to tell. The night little Kate, coming up on six years old and cute as a button, told her mother she'd find the old man at "21." The way he told the story, it was all about my ingenuity, my resourcefulness, my inside line to Daddy's glamorous nightlife. My mother had become a bit player in this story, the maid who takes phone calls, the babysitter who waits for the grownups to come home, a walk-on character in her own marriage.

"I thought that was you. The lady who makes movies." I whirled around to face Belhaloumi Jebel, with his glinting con-man smile and his cigarette breath. We were eye-to-eye, and his were so dark they seemed to be solid pupil. "Good to see you again. How are you enjoying Brussels?"

"Just fine."

"I regret the weather has not been more conducive."

"Don't give it a second thought."

"I'm glad you like our hotel."

"Don't you have work to do?"

"It can wait." He mounted the stool next to mine and wagged a finger at the bartender, pointing to my cup of espresso. He wanted one too.

I had nothing to say, no intentions beyond finishing my coffee. If I had had a newspaper, I would have buried my nose in it. I gave him a frosty shoulder, answering his questions with monosyllables, waiting for him to drift away, but when I heard the words "your husband" and "Lida" and "last night," I turned. "What did you say?"

"Did your husband tell you what he and Lida talked about at the bar last night?"

My foot had just slipped on another stair, and I couldn't quite reach the banister. "He did," I lied. I don't know if I averted my eyes, or if he noticed the blood surging to my cheeks. Had they arranged a tryst? If not that, what words had they dared exchange sitting three feet from me?

"You are a most understanding woman. I'm surprised you have come here today. You know, Lida is the sort of woman you have one drink with and then she thinks you are friends, though *you* are only an obstacle to her, like this—" He pretended to flick something off his shirt sleeve. "Last night after you left, she and her Russian friend had a long talk regarding you and your husband."

"What the hell do you want?"

"I'm trying to help you. I'm a translator and you have a problem, but perhaps you don't see it. Maybe you will be in Brussels tonight and we can meet again?"

I reached into my pants pocket for my franc notes and set two fifties on the counter as I slid off the stool.

"I am hoping you don't leave so soon. This is too much for coffee. Here, here." He tried to push a bill into my hand.

"Fuck off," I muttered, and pressed through a clutch of businessmen crowding the entrance. I didn't bolt the way I had last night. I didn't run through the lobby, didn't hit the pavement reeling, but I walked as fast as I could to the end of the block. I turned into a tabac at the corner and pointed to a pack of cigarettes behind the cash register, grabbing a box of matches from the counter. I had begun to tremble from the inside out, and I don't remember which way I walked when I left the tabac, or how far I got before hailing a cab. What could Mac have said to her? He tells me everything, confesses every wayward thought and fantasy, reports on all sorts of meetings and conversations. Except this one. I could have asked him last night in the cab. I came this close. He might have told me. Or maybe he'd have tinkered with that translation too.

I told the cabdriver to take me to my hotel. Mac would meet me at four-thirty on the Grand'Place. He'd show up, all right. He's always on time. Never misses an appointment. He would show up on time and do the other things he does so well: confess and explain, weasel his way out of this on moral grounds. She had a prior claim, after all, and count on Mac to do the right thing by the downtrodden, to weigh in on the side of the underdog, the poor girl stuck in the Soviet Union, in the one-room flat with her mother. He would meet me at four-thirty as he said he would, but I had no idea which way the bodies would fall. I rolled down the window. A rush of cold air for my nicotine vertigo. First cigarette in years. Of course it has come to this. He is my shooting star, my firefly, my deer on the road, in his nature always about to disappear. I wake in the middle of the night and listen for his breathing, I hold my hand to his back to feel the warm skin, the echo of his heartbeat against my palm. I have never really believed something so wonderful could last through the night, and at last I know I have been right all along.

I tapped the cabdriver on the shoulder. "Take me to the Galeries St.-Hubert." It was just around the corner from our hotel. The movie Eric had invited me to see would begin at one, and I had to catch him before the lights went down.

FOURTEEN

▼

There had been something Mac had wanted to tell her on his last night, his last few hours in Leningrad, the news had come over the telex late that afternoon, it would be in the newspapers everywhere but there the following day. He made her dinner, lamb chops and home-fried potatoes, and they drank the first of two bottles of wine, then they exchanged presents sitting on the living-room floor, like Christmas morning. She gave him a small, delicate watercolor a friend had made of the city, an aerial view of its bridges and canals and brightly painted buildings, with today's date penciled in the corner, June 30, 1974. He gave her a pair of purple knit gloves and a gift-wrapped box he said he had bought at the *beriozka*.

"How do you pronounce it?" she asked.

"Joy."

"Zjoy?"

"Ja-oy."

"Zjoy?"

"Yes, that's it, it's from France."

"What does it mean?"

"When you feel great happiness," he said in Russian, "that feeling is also called 'joy.' "

"What we feel."

"Yes."

"Excellent." She dabbed some on her wrist and held it to his nose.

"Oh," he said.

"What?"

"I thought it had a different scent, I thought it would be more—"

"I love it." She pressed her finger behind her ear and reached under her long peasant skirt, a spot of perfume for the top of her thigh.

"I'll open another bottle of wine," he said.

"What time is it now?"

"Eight."

"Four more hours."

They were trying so hard to be casual, to ignore the finality, the severity, of what was to happen.

"I didn't know they sold things from France in the *beriozka*."

"It wasn't much of a selection but I was surprised myself. Pass me your glass."

Though his plane was not leaving for Helsinki until five the next morning, he had to leave his flat, say goodbye to her, at midnight. The city's bridges started to open at two and some stayed open until five to handle all the ship traffic. At midnight he would drive to the consulate, where he had arranged to meet the consul general's driver, who would take him to the airport in time to return to the city before the bridges went up and the roads became impassable.

"It's too bad we couldn't have taken a trip to Yalta or Sochi."

He almost answered, "Maybe next time," but caught himself. "We would never have gotten permission to go so far."

"You're probably right. When I was thirteen, I was sent to Young Pioneer camp near Yalta. The mountains are very beautiful."

It would not be a breach of security for Mac to tell her the news that had come over the telex that afternoon. Security was not the reason for his silence. It was that he knew it would cause her pain, tonight of all nights, another reminder of the gates closing. The city was like Alcatraz, a beautiful spot on the water from which there was no escape. But if you were lucky enough to get across the border, they made sure you could never come back.

"What time is it now?" she asked.

"Eight-ten."

Three hours and fifty minutes. She lifted her skirt again, this time high enough that Mac could see she wore no underwear. "I am sorry," she said in Russian, "that my 'Zjoy' does not please you."

"But it does."

They left his building at midnight, she helped him carry his suitcases and a bag of souvenirs to his car. It was dark out— from midnight to one was the only hour of darkness during the White Nights—but the streetlights had not gone on yet. An almost pitch-black darkness, relieved every few minutes by the headlights of a passing car. Still, they were cautious reflexively, as they had always been in public. They had said goodbye upstairs, now she was valiant on the street, a stalwart Young Pioneer, full of enthusiasm and purpose. At the door to the car, they clutched hands, held themselves cheek-to-cheek. Then she drew back, looked him in the eye, and said—he had never heard her say this, didn't know she knew the word—*Ciao.* Like this was the last day of the season on Nantucket and they would be back next year for tennis and clambakes on the beach. Her eyes looked violet and forgiving in the glare of a passing headlight, and if she called him in six months or a year and said, It's me, I'm here, he might not be able to resist.

"*Ciao, bella,*" he said.

"I have already written you my first letter. It's up here." She pointed to the side of her head.

"You look very beautiful tonight."

"Because of you."

"Whatever happens, Lida—"

"You'll be late. The bridges will go up."

"Remember what I said."

"Always."

She waved with her purple gloves and smiled as he drove off, but he was sure he saw her face crumple in the reddish light cast by his taillights, in his rearview mirror on his way down Kirovski Prospekt. Then she was gone, like a ship out to sea. All of a sudden, there was no trace of her. He had drunk too much, and reminded himself to drive with particular care. Not so tough on an empty street, empty like a parking lot with no cars. Empty. Except for the familiar beige Lada behind him. Not a trace of her anywhere. Except here. Mac pressed the fingers of his right hand to his nostrils.

He spent the next day in Helsinki, at a hotel near the airport, waiting for the twice-weekly Pan Am flight that evening to Washington. He showered and drifted in and out of sleep for hours, exhausted, hung over—welcome anesthesia for the shock of being without her. At noon he ordered breakfast from room service and slept again before it arrived. He spoke to her in his dreams and in his half sleep, reaching for the pillow beside him. It is possible, he said to her in Russian, to love two women at once but in different ways. He turned over and called room service again, asked if they could send up the *International Herald Tribune* with his breakfast. It was not until he saw the front page of the paper that he remembered what he had decided against telling her in Leningrad. BAR-YSHNIKOV DEFECTS, read the headline just below the fold, ON BALLET TOUR. Dateline: Ottawa.

As members of the ballet company walked toward a charter bus to return to their hotel after their last performance in Toronto, Mr. Baryshnikov suddenly turned toward a waiting car. Though pursued by the KGB, the Soviet security apparatus, Canadian police assisted him into the car, which then left for an undisclosed location.

▼

FIFTEEN

I found him in the dark, so low down in an aisle seat he was nearly supine. "Hey, you made it," he whispered. He straightened up and swung his knees to one side to let me pass. "Just started. You haven't missed a thing."

"I can't stay." I squatted by his armrest, watching his face flicker in and out of darkness to a sound track that sounded like Wynton Marsalis with an overlay of soft female French. I could pick up every fourth or fifth word. "I need your help."

"This minute?"

"Yeah."

"It can't wait?"

"Shhhhhhh," someone hissed. "*Tais-toi!*"

"It can't wait."

I wanted to tell him, I had meant to tell him, but when he took my arm in the theater lobby and asked what was wrong, all I said was "What did you get on film?"

"Of Mac and Lida? Nothing that'll win the Palme d'Or. Talking on a park bench, horsing around on the street, sitting around a pastry shop until they split. Mac still has the tape deck."

"Give me mood."

"Raining, gray, melancholy."

"They were melancholy?"

"The weather was melancholy. They were—"

"They were what?"

"Can we pick this up after? I don't know if you saw the marquee, but this isn't a three-day screening of *Berlin Alexanderplatz*. It's a little French number, eighty minutes long. I want to get my money's worth."

"Wait." I held on to his sleeve with a fierceness that surprised me. I was imagining what I might do left alone for the next three hours—what Lida had done all day yesterday: stalk every hotel in Brussels. "I need you to give me a hand." I was improvising, and so jittery I thought my teeth might start to chatter. "I have to call Mrs. Kazes in Istanbul and make sure we're still scheduled to interview her in the synagogue tomorrow afternoon. And call the rabbi and confirm everything at his end. It may take an hour to get through. Then we need to go over locations and the sequences to pick up."

"I'll be out of here in an hour."

"That's not enough time."

"It's plenty, Kate."

"We start shooting in less than twenty-four hours. I've gone through a pack of Tums this morning. I'm a wreck."

"All right," he sighed. "What's the plan?"

He followed me out of the theater and into the arcade, and it seemed as if every sound echoed in my ears. Things were coming in too clearly, too loud. "Takeout for lunch, run through the schedule, and hit the phones."

"Have you been in here before?" He meant the majestic Galeries St.-Hubert we were walking through, a scaled-down Champs Elysées, a window shopper's paradise beneath a three-story barrel-vault glass roof that would have let in enough light to read by if the sun had been shining. The shop windows were breathtaking, each one a brilliant, miniature stage set. There were hundred-dollar umbrellas for sale, handmade lace baby bibs, Italian driving gloves, chocolates as dazzling as diamonds. The heels of women's shoes clicked against the stone walkway, and voices rose and fell like birdcalls in half a dozen languages. "It was the first closed shopping arcade in Europe. Eighteen-forty-something. The mother of all malls."

"What about Mac and Lida?"

"What do you want to know?"

"The bottom line."

"She's a strange duck." We left the arcade and turned the corner onto the small plaza we had first come upon last night. It looked more foreign today, as if someone had been fiddling with the color controls, sharpening outlines, deepening hues. A forest after a month of rain when the moss is swollen, gravid, about to burst. A cityscape painted by a Superrealist. "When she's with Mac, she has a needy quality, like if she lets go, he'll bolt. But when he's not around, she's five hundred watts of halogen. We can get a decent sandwich in here. How're your francs holding out?"

"She clings to him?"

"Like Velcro. You hear a fuzzy ripping sound when she lets go. A sort of postcoup détente. How long were they an item?"

"Three weeks."

"No wonder they still have that starry-eyed glow. What do you want to eat?"

Had I sent Eric with them this morning to take pictures of her clinging? No. I had wanted the camera to chaperon. I had hoped it would inhibit her, the way I had expected my presence to restrain her last night. But she kept fooling me, or I kept fooling myself: I expected her behavior to make sense, to proceed from promontories I understood, to recognize certain boundaries that translated from one language to another, like international road sign symbols: a red circle bisected with a diagonal slash means NO PARKING. A man traveling with his wife is not up for grabs. Or is he? He'd never throw it away on a bimbo or even my best friend, but Lida's claim was somewhat out of the ordinary. And her interest in Mac was off the charts.

"How's ham and cheese on a baguette?" Eric asked.

"Fine. I'll see if there's any cold beer."

"Make it Stella or Vieux-Temps. By the way"—Eric sidled up to me at the end of the sandwich counter—"if she and Mac hadn't talked to each other in seventeen years, how did she know we'd be in Brussels last night?"

"She has a great travel agent."

I was still trying to connect the dots between the woman Mac knew back then and the Lida I had met last night. In Leningrad she hadn't cared that she was breaking every rule in the book, and that it might cost her dearly. She still didn't. The cellular phone was a recent acquisition, but the bravado was vintage, honed to an extravagant pitch in all her years in the West.

I am accustomed to working long hours on tight deadlines, under so much pressure that my neck muscles ache and my temper tends to flare, and to Eric I must have seemed very nearly myself as I scarfed down my sandwich and drank a few beers, Eric in the armchair by the window of my hotel room while I sat in the center of the bed, surrounded by papers and brown bags, the morning newspaper, the files, the telephone, and an ashtray. I was almost myself: the busywork had redirected my attention and the beer had made its way to my central nervous system. "Let's go through the locations for the next three days—here's a copy—and see if they still make sense."

"Let me crack open the window. The cigarette smoke—"

"Sure, sure. We have the synagogue tomorrow from noon to four. We set up from noon to one. Mrs. Kazes arrives at twelve-thirty, I talk to her for half an hour, explain the drill, run through the questions we've agreed on—"

"Looks fine to me. All the locations look fine, Kate. You know what you're doing, you don't need me to—"

"What's our backup if Daniel is late? He's supposed to get in at midnight but what if—"

"We rent a Nagra for a day. This happened to me once in Prague. It took half a dozen phone calls. What else do you want to worry about?"

"Hey, look."

"What?"

"It's snowing." I got up and stood by the window.

"Flurries. It'll never stick, it's too wet."

I was looking over the tarred rooftops and the loopy, lovely Baroque gables perched at their front ends, set there like medallions on the hoods of cars. The plaza below was crowded with lunchtime traffic, a sea of rain slickers, trenchcoats, umbrellas opening one by one against the wet snow.

"Where did you live when you lived here?"

"On the other side of the Grand'Place. A flat about as big as this room. All I had was a Steenbeck and a bed."

"And an eighteen-year-old Laotian girl."

"Not a regular feature. She just came up in the afternoons on her break from the Chinese grocery downstairs."

"And made you lemon-grass tea, and walked on your back. 'So petite and delicate you thought her little fingers would break.'"

"I sure did." Eric laughed. "For weeks I bought bok choy every day, just so I could watch her ring it up at the cash register. She finally said to me, 'Every day bok choy. What you do so much?' I invited her up to see. The refrigerator was packed with wilting bok choy. She didn't understand at first. Then she did."

I had my eye on a party of pedestrians meandering across the square the way a river runs. "Did you lick her all over?"

"Sorry?"

"A French photographer once told me that Vietnamese women are so soft you can lick them all over."

"Are we still working or is this recess?"

Is it possible to spot your husband six stories down crossing a street arm in arm with another woman? Or is it another man in a navy-blue jacket, a navy wool cap, beside a tall woman in a beige coat? I am farsighted, I can make out the neon words in every shop window along the plaza and a jacket the color of Mac's, but this couple is walking away from me at a steady clip, about to turn a corner. Then they are gone from the screen, from my view through this windowpane. Run it back. In slow motion. "Is there another beer in that bag?"

"We went through all of it."

"Shit."

"I've got something apropos in my room. I picked it up in the duty free. Sit tight."

I didn't move from the window, I pressed my nose against it, hoping to see them again, because every sighting was evidence that I could trust my eyes and my instincts. Evidence that I had not been had by Belhaloumi Jebel. But there was no sign of Mac or Lida, and I wandered down the hall into Eric's room to get the drink he had promised me, and maybe for a second opinion, if I could bear to tell him what I had been through in the last few hours. I saw him kneeling in the corner of his room, rifling through his knapsack with his back to me. I'd start at the beginning, tell him everything I couldn't bring myself to tell Mac last night. He had heard me coming. "Are you ready for this? I'm going to make you a Black Russian. I bought Kahlúa and Stolichnaya as presents for a Turkish pal. Remember the guy we had dinner with our first night there last summer? But I buried them so well I can't find them."

I came up from behind and started to laugh. "You sure you weren't in cahoots with Lida's travel agent?"

"I'd rather be in cahoots with Lida when she starts importing talk-dirty-to-me phone calls to Mother Russia."

His room was half the size of mine, not much wider than the narrow cot against the wall. A small round window, like a porthole or a huge eye, peered down at us and witnessed me lay my hands on his shoulders. They are broad and the muscles are as firm as bone; cameramen are like mountain climbers, built to hump, as Eric sometimes says. Built to carry. We had been lovers ten years before, two nights of daiquiri-induced groping in his downtown loft, a colossal failure to ignite, and all these years of working together, five or six projects in a decade. We were only occasional confidants. He had told me about the Laotian girl in Brussels in the mid-seventies, and I had told him once, without mentioning his name, about B.J.

I could feel his muscles flinch under my fingers. "I must have missed a transition," he said, still kneeling. I moved my hands toward the back of his neck, kneading the skin through layers of winter clothes. My thumbs met at his hairline, and he let his head relax and drop back against my breasts. His eyes were closed, his face placid as if he were a man asleep. Even guilty pleasure is pleasure. When he spoke it was a whisper. "Don't do this to me, Kate." You might mistake it for coaxing: no means yes.

"Do what?"

"Put me in the middle."

"I thought you were an adventurer. High-risk investments. Skydiving. Footage from the eye of the storm."

I had slipped my hands around to his chin, his cheeks, stroking the temples with my thumb. My own pleasure surprised me, and my willingness. I bent down and put my lips against his and held them there for a moment. Had I sought him out at the movie theater with this in mind all along? I kissed his forehead, ran my fingers through his scalp, I did what I like done to me. I kissed his ears, lightly, as light as the snow flurries, and reached to unbutton his shirt. I had walked down the hall for this, but Lida had come all the way from Paris. Would she succeed? Mac had said he wouldn't and I trusted him, or I thought I did, or I had until last night. Is trust a constant, like the force of gravity, or is it contingent, forever in flux, like a tropical storm, susceptible to a butterfly flapping its wings in China?

"It just seems that way from a distance," Eric said softly. "Up close I'm a terrible coward."

"But you feel very good right now."

"So do you."

I am not petite and doll-like, not soft all over, but I imagined Eric thinking of the Laotian girl as he held me, I was sure she was responsible for some of this ardor. It was the least I could do, mentioning her, luring him back to her. I unbuttoned his shirt and untucked the silky long-sleeved undershirt from inside his pants so I could feel the warm flesh of his waist. We stumbled toward the bed and landed on it laughing. Nervous laughter. Guilty laughter. I was out of practice. I was trying to let go, to switch off the part of my brain that tells me what to do next. The bedroom door was ajar. A straight shot to the elevator. Mac could see us if he was there, and isn't that what I wanted? Take that and that and that. Take my picture, I almost said to Eric. Get it all on tape. Tell me the place is bugged. Remind me of the danger. Let me break the rules before they break me first, the way Lida does. A hotel room is the most treacherous country of all.

I extended my leg and kicked the door shut, his room was that small.

I undid buttons and zippers and clothing fell away, it wrinkled and snagged between the bedding and our skin. I hadn't expected his tenderness, the way he cupped my face in both hands and whispered my name three or four times, I thought it was love talk, and I hadn't expected that either, my name all those times so softly and holding me to him, and the way he said, "You're shivering."

But I wasn't.

He held me tighter and whispered, "Let's not, okay, Kate?"

He could feel me nodding my head, and that was when he pulled back and looked at me. "Hey, kiddo, you should have taken me up on the Black Russian, you wouldn't feel a thing

now . . . This is nothing to cry over, believe me . . . Come
here . . . I'm not turning you away, you can stay as long as
you want, but I need to put my clothes back on . . . You too
. . . Joints like this, there's too much heat or there's none.
No goddamn Kleenexes either . . . Here, take this. It's not
ironed but it's clean . . . Next time we stay at the Hilton.
You've got to get on the gravy train. You want to be the
producer of choice for the crack dealers when they make their
training videos. How to market, keep records, build a client
base, cultivate media contacts. You do one or two of those a
year and no more of these bring-your-own-shower-cap hotels
. . . Let me open the Stoly. You want it with or without the
Kahlúa? Speaking of ironing, what was that story you told a
long time ago about your boyfriend in Cuernavaca who wanted
you to learn to iron?"

"Don't cajole me like I'm dying." I turned my head away
as I pulled my pants up from around my ankles. I was going
to pull on my turtleneck, apologize, and get out of there fast.

"I never saw you cry, that's all. I had no idea you were so
upset about her. I thought you were more nervous about the
shoot. When all this started in here—I wasn't thinking clearly,
I thought you wanted a drink, a little TLC. I didn't understand
you were serious. Until just now. Hey, Kate, you don't have
to run away. Not from me." He was standing in the corner
by the knapsack, and I was standing as far away as I could,
about four feet, turning away from him as I tucked my shirt
into my pants.

"Do you see my sweater?"

"Relax a minute. This isn't junior high."

From behind me, I felt his hand on the back of my neck
and I tried to do what he said. I took a deep breath and let it
out slowly, and slowly I turned and let him wrap his arms

around me. I closed my eyes and let my cheek fall against his shoulder. I still wanted to flee, but I was trying to do what he said, to catch my breath, take it easy, relax, because I couldn't think of what else to do. "I'm not very good at being embarrassed," I said softly.

"No one is. That's why it's embarrassing."

"This isn't part of your job description."

"You'd be surprised the things cameramen are called on to do. We're not protected by ordinary labor laws. Like minimum wage." He laughed and I laughed and our arms dropped away from each other and it wasn't nearly as awkward as it had been two minutes before.

"Since you asked, I'll take the vodka with Kahlúa in it, please."

"Have a seat. Coming right up. Did you happen to notice an ice machine in the hallway of this glorious motor lodge?"

A moment later, he turned and handed me a cheap hotel glass half filled with what looked like dark-brown ink. He seemed remarkably unruffled, a gracious host making do with limited supplies. We took proper places on the bed, sitting at either end like bookends, and passed the Black Russian back and forth, because it was in the only glass he had. I felt like someone coming out of surgery, groggy, a little needy, a little dull.

"She's a piece of work, Kate. She's a handful. But once we left her hotel last night, I assumed you and Mac had worked things out. I figured you understood each other. When you asked me to follow them around today, I thought you really wanted footage for a project. I didn't understand that you wanted me to chaperon."

"Until when?"

"Just now. When we were—" He wiggled his forefinger

back and forth in the space between us. "What's so funny?"

"You know that Faulkner story from his days in Hollywood? The director says to him, 'You're the writer. How do we convey to the audience that this man and this woman have slept together?' 'Easy,' he says. 'Make them brother and sister.' "

"That's good."

"I just remembered I didn't get through to the rabbi in Istanbul. I got Mrs. Kazes but there was no answer at his house." I handed Eric the drink and stood up. I would call Turkey and maybe Nan in New York. "If I have another sip, I'll collapse." I started to say that I'd only gotten a few hours of sleep last night, but I didn't want to bring the conversation back to Lida and the way she had managed to put so much distance between Mac and me.

"Don't forget your room key."

"Thanks."

"Is it still four-thirty on the Grand'Place?"

"Yes." I had my hand on the doorknob, about to swing it open, when he spoke again.

"Look, Kate—"

He sounded serious and somewhat alarmed. I turned to face him with a sense of dread. "What is it now?"

"You can take the sixty-two dollars out of my paycheck, but next time let's change planes in Frankfurt."

I smiled and tried to look into his eyes without turning away, without bolting. They are dark green, and his nose is long and straight, and when I first knew him, his jet-black hair came down to his shoulders. Now he wears it in an austere, punkish crewcut that exaggerates all his otherwise unremarkable features and seems to make his scalp glow in certain lights. I remember standing there for three or four seconds, enjoying his gentle barb, his strange good looks, and thinking how much

I liked him, and how rarely I really looked at him, but thinking that if I lost Mac in all of this, it wouldn't be Eric I would run to again for consolation. I would want someone who needed me a little more, someone I could imagine longing for.

"It's a deal," I said to Eric, and opened the door and stepped into the corridor, pulling it shut behind me. I took two steps and looked down, I remembered to breathe deeply, take it easy, take it slow. When I looked up, I stopped in my tracks. Mac stood fifteen feet down the hall, on his way out of our room. As soon as he turned around, he would see me. There was no open doorway to duck into, no L-shaped corridor to run toward, no looking glass to step through, and the doors to every room, the door I had just pulled shut, lock automatically. So I stood and waited. I would not have long to wait. He had my Nikon slung over his shoulder, and he was pulling closed our door, on the verge of turning around. But when he saw me a second later, he did not say what I was sure he would. "Did you see what's going on in there? Cigarettes and beer bottles all over the place. Nothing seems to be missing, but I'm going downstairs to raise hell. This is—"

But he stopped when he saw I wasn't moving from outside Eric's door, when he saw what a mess I was. "What happened?"

"Nothing."

"Are you all right?"

"Uh-huh."

He pointed to the door to our room, and there was a question or two in the gesture. Did I know what had happened in there? Any connection between my disheveled state and the room's?

"The cigarettes are mine," I said, without moving any closer to him. "Eric and I were having lunch." I felt disoriented, as if I were seeing Mac through the wrong end of the binoculars. I wanted to close my eyes and wake up in the recovery room, open my eyes in another country. The corridor felt like a poorly lighted tunnel, lined with numbered doors that led to rooms as small as Eric's and to every sort of danger. Mac looked me up and down and settled on my face, my swollen eyes. Was his guilt as obvious as I had imagined it would be? Or was his frightened, hesitant gaze only a response to evidence of my treachery? I don't just mean the cigarettes and beer bottles, I mean the whole tawdry package, down to my bare feet. I had just realized I'd left my socks in Eric's room.

I don't know how long we stood that way, at opposite ends of the hall like duelists who know they'd be better off talking things over, but every second we didn't talk, we lost ground, we lost hope, we died a little and then a little more. Beads of sweat formed along his hairline, and his eyes dropped to my feet again, for confirmation. He was putting it all together, the pieces of a grisly crime. I'd been fucking Eric all along. I shook my head no, but he was still gaping at my feet and biting his upper lip.

There was a sudden clanging noise, the commotion of metal meeting metal, that sounded like a car ferry docking. A few seconds later, the elevator door swung open on a right-hand hinge, so that the door hid whoever was there from me but not from Mac. "What happens? I am wait, wait, how long time. You finded camera?"

It was Lida's unmistakable voice, and when she let the door swing shut behind her and strode, her back to me, toward Mac, maybe to get a look at the camera, he shook his head and held up his hand like a traffic cop. "Say hello to Kate," he said.

"Who?"

Mac turned Lida around by the shoulders of her trenchcoat to face me at the other end of the hall, and I was startled all over again at her titanic presence. "Mac tells me you go to Bruges all the day." Her trenchcoat was tied tight at the waist, open at the collar, the layers beneath shrouding and adding bulk to her middle-age spread. There was nothing fancy or ostentatious about her, except her unkempt Amazon beauty, and her eyes, a brilliant azure even in the dreary light of the corridor.

"I changed my mind."

She turned back to Mac and said something in Russian.

He held up the Nikon for her to see.

"Good, we make picture. Then Karlis house for Russian lunch."

"Kate, do you want to come?"

I heard a door click open behind me and then Eric mutter "Jesus Christ" under his breath as he took stock of what he'd come upon. I turned and saw a handful of my black kneesocks in his fist, which he twisted around behind him, back behind the door to his room, and dropped. "Well, the gang's all here!" he said brightly, and stepped into the hall, into the eye of the storm.

"What happens movie of my life? Come, we eat good Russian lunch with Karlis and you make movie."

I could see Eric glance at Mac, and Mac look Eric up and down the way he had me, but in a matter of seconds, we were all looking at Lida. "Karlis good friend of mine's," she said to Eric. "Good guy. You will like." I remembered what Belhaloumi Jebel had said about what it takes to be a friend of Lida's.

"Sounds terrific," Eric said. "And there'll be borscht for everyone? Come in here and help me carry the mag case."

Lida followed Eric into his room, and I had a feeling it was
to leave me alone with Mac for a few minutes, so I could
explain myself and get Eric off the hook.

"I thought you were going to Bruges," Mac said.

"I had to call some people in Turkey. Arrangements for
tomorrow."

"Are you all set?"

I nodded, though I wasn't quite sure he meant set for Turkey, and I had a feeling I wasn't anymore.

"Did you see much of the city?" Mac asked.

"A little. It started to snow. Then stopped." I didn't think
there was anything else I had seen all day that I was ready to
talk to him about.

"I must have missed that," he said. I kept waiting for him
to get on with his confession, his tortured, Jesuitical justifi-
cation for what he had done or would do with Lida, to get it
over with, so that I could proceed with mine. But there was
nothing in his expression that suggested he was about to speak.
He just looked at me—we were six or eight feet from one
another now, narrowing the gap—the way he does sometimes
on Sam's birthday or on the anniversary of the day he died,
like he still can't believe that what happened really happened.
I must have been looking at him the same way, shattered but
still standing, trying to make sense of a loss too huge for words.

SIXTEEN

T here is no sign of Mac and me in this next clip, just Lida and Karlis walking across the Grand'Place, an occasional straggler casting a sidelong glance at the camera, and the ancient square's guild houses rising up behind them like a glorious mountain range. There are so many gold-coated surfaces, so many ledges and roofs crowded with Baroque lions, warriors, trumpeters as delicate as Giacometti's figures, but not nearly as lonely. On the Steenbeck screen, the square is as delectable as a Fabergé egg, but when we walked across it that afternoon, on the heels of Lida's strange friend and his blue-eyed dog, it had a menacing, hallucinatory quality, as if we were seeing it through an opiate that made every figure, every stone animal carving, so real I could imagine them slinking toward me. We were in Fellini's hands, or Dante's, shaken by our meeting in the hotel and relieved that all we had to do now was follow Karlis, almost a head taller than Lida, marking the way with his broad-brimmed black hat and a steady plume of cigarette smoke.

There had been no formal introductions, we'd just attached ourselves to the two of them outside the hotel and started moving, with no more sense of purpose or destination than the wind. I knew somehow that the unleashed Siberian husky loping along beside Mac and me, as sleek and solid as a wolf, belonged to Lida's friend, but I wasn't sure who the rest of us belonged to anymore. It was as if I were made of glass or gossamer or dust, and I didn't know how much more pressure I could take without coming apart. Maybe I already had. We turned off the Grand'Place onto a street so narrow the sun must not have shone there in centuries, and I marshaled the courage to ask Mac where we were going.

"With him," he snapped.

"But why?"

"Why not?"

We were ten or twelve paces behind Lida and Eric and Karlis, listening to her laughter, to fragments of the Russian she spoke with Karlis, and the boisterous, fractured English she reserved for Eric. I made out a word here and there but I was paying more attention to appearances. Eric had cut off the camera, looped an arm through hers, and begun telling her the three-part joke about the dog, the brick, and the cigar with the punchline I can never remember. There was, in all of his gestures and intonations toward her, an exaggerated interest that if you didn't know him, you might mistake for the real thing. Was this performance for Mac, reassurance that what had looked like our fling was over and done with, and he was the same old Eric he'd been before, the irrepressible but harmless flirt, the cameraman happily married to his instrument? I'd heard a Southern woman once described as "everyone's pal and nobody's gal." I'd often thought of Eric as her counterpart, but I couldn't help feeling left out now, the way I had last night; he had shunned me for her, and maybe Mac had too. I looked to see what was on Mac's face, but he averted his eyes and feigned interest in a window display of white chocolate reindeer in a Christmas diorama. He hadn't slept with her. I think that's the moment I realized it. If he had, he wouldn't be so wounded now, so furious, smoldering in silence. He'd have understood what I had done, what it looked like I had done, as simple retaliation. He might even have welcomed it; it would have made us even. I moved closer to him, an inch toward reconciliation, opened my hand, and brushed my pinkie against his. He pulled away, but gently, almost inconspicuously, the way you do when you don't want your retreat to be received as abrupt. I wanted so badly to make things right that three or four times I started to say, "I'm sorry, Sparks, I'm really sorry," but I was afraid anything I said would be held against me, terrified that when it was time to go to the airport, Mac would play the card he knew would crush me. So we kept going on our reluctant pilgrimage, to a Russian meal none of us wanted, following a man whose hat I had seen more of than his face.

On the Steenbeck screen, he and Lida are Beauty and the Beast. Imagine an aging Raskolnikov on a good day. He's thin as a stick, with a scraggly mustache and the sunken chest and cheeks of a failed artist. His nose is grotesquely hooked, like a demonic creature from Hieronymus Bosch, but his eyes are big and brown and fixed on Lida. He's wearing a threadbare black dinner jacket, bright-red wool scarf, and a broad-brimmed black hat, dragging hard on a hand-rolled cigarette, the smoke pouring in great clouds from his mouth, his enlarged nostrils. A man with a sense of style and pedigree and no money at all. It's hard to tell if he's seventy or a fifty-year-old with prematurely gray hair. An eccentric, in any case, a lost Russian soul roaming the tangled streets of the dainty, bourgeois city with a dog bred for the Siberian tundra and a woman still full of surprises for all of us.

"You have a picture of her?" I overheard Eric ask Lida. We had followed Karlis past the Bourse and into a seamier part of town, a far cry from the Church of the Very Well Dressed. A bustling, bazaar-like street closed to traffic swarmed with ordinary Belgians hunting down bargains in the cut-rate clothing stores, on the circular racks jammed with winter coats, in the enormous bins of boots, shoes, blank cassette tapes that lined the sidewalks like pushcarts.

"Of course. What kind mama with no picture?" Lida began digging through her handbag. "I show photos to Mac in café. I tell all stories of Sonya. Champion swimmer. Wins much prize."

"She looks just like you," he said.

"Everybody say so. Mac too. 'Just like mama.' "

Karlis stopped to light a cigarette and the rest of us slowed down. I'd thought at first that he looked sinister, but as he stood before a window of toy trains, with a bony hand cupped around his flickering match, eyes closed, sucking on the cigarette like a mournful saxophone player, I felt sorry for him. His clothes were thin and wrinkled, and he was built so flimsily it was surprising his dog was handsome and robust. Lida sashayed to Mac's side and said something softly in Russian. The two of them laughed as I looked at my watch. It was three-forty-five, and I realized it was the first time I had seen them talking since we had met in the corridor. They talked easily, too easily. He had saved all his warmth for her. Had they been avoiding one another so diligently because they'd slept together? Or had they only gone as far as Eric and I had?

"What's so funny?" Eric asked them.

Mac's English translation was as soft as Lida's Russian had been. "She said he's just like an artist. Poor as can be but he expects everyone to buy his pictures so they'll be rich when he dies."

"Who are you talking about?"

"Karlis." Had the stranger heard his name mentioned? He looked over and waved us on but didn't wait for us to catch up. It was as if he wanted to keep his distance. "Lida said she thought about buying a painting at the exhibit but she couldn't find one that wouldn't give her nightmares."

"What exhibit?" Eric asked.

"He took us to see a show of his work at a bank across the street from the Bourse. Now he's taking us to see his restorations, and for a bite to eat. He works for the Musées des Beaux-Arts. Lida has a canvas in Paris he said he'd help her restore."

"What time did you see the exhibit?" I asked.

"About an hour ago."

An hour ago, I thought I'd seen Mac and Lida from my hotel window. Maybe it hadn't been them after all. Surely I'd have noticed a character like Karlis if he'd been anywhere nearby, even six floors down. At the corner, Karlis signaled our route with another broad wave. We crossed a boulevard and found ourselves on a quiet, tree-lined side street, row houses and two young mothers pushing strollers into the twilight. Karlis and the dog rambled five paces ahead of me. At my back, Lida was telling Mac a joke in Russian that he translated, line by line, into English for Eric. I dug my hands into the pockets of my jacket and watched a car stop in the middle of the block to let a man with a Yankees baseball cap cross the street. There was nothing menacing or hypnotic or hallucinatory about the street, the moment, the bunch of us ambling down the sidewalk, maintaining the appearance that we were friends. I wasn't afraid anymore, or maybe I was too exhausted to absorb another particle of fear. I wouldn't have known where to carry it.

"Not lotion," I heard Eric say. "Laotian. Laos. A country near Cambodia . . . So delicate I thought her little fingers would break off if I held them too tight . . . About this tall . . . Mac, I thought you'd heard me tell this story . . . Jesus, look where your friend is taking us. You know this guy from Leningrad?"

I didn't think Mac had ever heard Eric tell the Laotian girl story; I'd only heard it once myself, a few years ago. Was Eric still doing penance, still trying to convince Mac that I wasn't really his type? Or did he just mean to reroute the sexual energy in the air, keep the ions bouncing between himself and Lida as a public service to me?

"We meet by café," Lida said. "He overlistens us speak Russian and wants talk. He have no one in Brussels for to talk to, only dog. Displace-ed person after war. From Latvia."

"What war?" Eric asked.

"World War. Of course."

"He hasn't found anyone to talk to in forty-five years?"

"I don't see anything out of the ordinary," Mac said, surveying the street up ahead. There was not much to see. It was another quiet side street, but no trees lined this one, and there were no young mothers pushing baby carriages. Dreary four- and five-story row houses, a string of parked cars, a construction

site, a bright-red billboard advertising cigarettes. And Karlis's
scarf, another speck of red in the distance, as he waited for us
on the curb across the street and flicked a cigarette butt into
the gutter.

"The street we're on is called the rue du Cirque," Eric said,
"for reasons that become obvious when the sun goes down.
They don't turn on the bright lights until then, and it only
ever looks like a Sunday hobby next to Times Square, but it's
all they've got."

The strip looked to be two or three blocks long, if you could
call it a strip. There were no movie marquees, no flashing
lights, no blinking neon, just a few sleazy storefront murals,
gigantic, bosomy drawings of women with eight-button gloves
and no pubic hair, and a few hand-painted signs in darkened
windows that said TOPLESS GIRLS, and SEXY VIDEO BAR. But
halfway down the block, in a lace-curtained storefront window
on a riser five feet high, sat a real naked woman in a wicker
armchair, talking on a telephone. One leg was crossed over
the other and she held the receiver against her cheek and
moved her lips, but with so little interest she might have been
talking to her dentist about the date of her next appointment.
Maybe she was. Her eyes had the spooky, unfocused glaze of
the blind, as if she'd taught herself the aerialist's mantra: Don't
look down. "She must have quite a phone bill," Eric said.

The window was trimmed with American Express decals,
Diners Club, MasterCard, Visa, the furbelows of instant grat-
ification, and reflected in it, superimposed on her belly, was
a hot-pink neon sign from across the street that said LE FRENCH.
For a moment I thought she had outlined the veins on her
breasts in blue, the way women did in ancient Egypt, but
when I moved closer I saw it was the veins themselves, the
blue-gray wild rivers of her breasts. Her nipples looked as hard

as stone. Her soft dark hair hid most of the phone receiver, but I didn't see any wires that suggested it worked. Like the phone I had tried to use in Lida's hotel last night: it held out hope, the illusion of rescue, the cunning shape of intimacy. When she dropped the receiver into the cradle on the end table—was the call over? had it ever begun?—she lost the blindman's gaze for a moment and saw me. I do not want to make the moment more than it was, to invest it with romanticism or tragedy or revelation. The truth is, I was thinking only of myself, and when she looked at me—really, it was two or three seconds at most—all that happened was I understood I was not the only one of us in pain.

I turned and kept walking, listening to Mac's footsteps behind me. Was he wondering what the hell we were doing here, the way I was, or had he racked this up as another detour on our lifelong journey to the seashore?

"I don't think I've ever heard the story of Eric's Laotian girlfriend," he said, and caught up with me. "Have you?"

"There's not much to it, from what I remember."

I knew that when Eric prodded Mac about his possible CIA connections, Mac could do mock-guilt. But could he do mock-innocence, and was this it, this bright effort to make conversation? Or was it his way of telling me he understood what had happened between Eric and me; he understood Eric was not a serious contender for my heart. Or maybe Mac had brought up the Laotian girl because she was safe. She'd become our in-house turn-on, our communal distraction, trotted out every twenty minutes to lure us away from what was really going on. As safe and titillating as the woman pretending to talk on the telephone and the nude drawings on storefront murals that lined this street like billboards. Eric might have photographs of her at home, so we'd know exactly how gorgeous and fragile her little fingers really were, but this wasn't a beauty pageant; we just needed the idea of her to keep us going. She was another beautiful exile from the Cold War, the Southeast Asian branch, who had found an American man who would never be there for her. She was our international heart throb, our poster child. You can send twenty dollars a month or you can turn the page. "The short version," I said to Mac, "is that they didn't get married and move to Levittown."

I didn't look at Mac but I could imagine him stung by my sarcasm, my mounting ire, the closer we came to the others, who stood waiting under a canary-yellow canopy that said VIDEO PEEP. "Please to follow me," Karlis said, and pulled open the matching yellow metal door. If I had been last in line, I might have bolted, but Mac was behind me and showed no signs of faintheartedness. Or else he was too preoccupied with his own wounds to allow in a portion of dread at where we were headed. I braced for a porno pantechnicon, go-go dancers in cages, panting men at the metal bars. But it was only an apartment building, a long, dimly lit hallway lined with wooden doors, the air saturated with musky incense and frying pork chops.

"Who lives here again?" Eric asked.

"I think we're going to visit a little old lady," I said, "who makes lace against her will." But what was I doing here against my own? I stopped halfway up the stairs and reached for Mac's arm. I had had enough of whatever this was. "Sparks," I said, but I didn't know what would come next.

"What?"

"Hold on a minute."

"What's wrong?" We stood together on a narrow linoleum step, in a stairwell painted dark brown and lit with twenty-five-watt bulbs that gave off a sinister yellow glow. "What is it?" he asked again.

"What it looked like—at our hotel—it didn't happen."

I shouldn't have reminded him. He sighed, a deep, unforgiving breath, an exhalation that took me by surprise, then turned and kept going up the stairs.

"Don't you believe me?"

"We'll talk about it later."

I didn't move, except to lean back and steady myself against the wall. It was not possible he would really punish me for this. There was only an hour before we left for the airport. I raced after him, up the stairs and down the hall to the only open door. I stuck my head in and was only a few inches from Mac's shoulder. It was a tiny room whose high ceiling was veined with cracks like a shattered windshield; a homemade loft bed covered with grotty bedsheets took up most of the floor space. There was barely room for the five of us to turn around. Books and magazines were stacked in piles about to topple over, and the buzz of Karlis's Russian, Lida's drumlike laughter, and a French-speaking newscaster burbling on an old black-and-white TV nearly drove me back into the hall. The place stank of cigarettes and oil paint and wet dog. The husky lowered his head into a metal water bowl in the corner and slurped while the radiator hissed and clanged. I followed the wire in an electric outlet from the wall to a hot plate on a stack of wooden milk crates. This was not the home of a man who restores paintings for the Musées des Beaux-Arts, and if he was planning to whip up a Russian meal for us, it would be bottled borscht and this morning's porridge.

"Come in," Karlis said to me, and pointed to something on the far wall, gesturing to Lida. "Maybe this you like to buy." She turned around to look at a small ugly painting of a mangled

bird and nodded without enthusiasm. The wall was covered
with such paintings, dark, amateurish, full of dead animals,
eyeballs, houses on fire, even a few melting clock faces. Lida
understood now that Karlis wasn't the man to help restore her
canvas. He raised his finger, motioning for us to follow, and
yanked aside a moth-eaten burgundy velvet drapery, a castoff
from an old movie theater, leading us through the doorway it
covered into another tiny room adjacent to the first, this one
filled with—I looked from floor to ceiling—more junk for
sale. Unfinished paintings, dusty odds and ends: a wooden
easel, an empty birdcage modeled on a pagoda, a cigar box of
coins, medallions, military ribbons, the head of a female mannequin leaning on its ear, a Little Black Sambo lead doorstop,
a freestanding metal cabinet that Karlis opened and took something out of with great care. He turned and presented it to
Lida, a tarnished silver samovar that he held up under ebony
handles, the way you lift a child under the armpits. "This you
will like."

Lida stepped forward to examine it as I looked at my watch.
Then I raised my arm and showed it to Mac. "We've got to
be out of the hotel by—"

"I know," he said, but did not move.

"Maybe I buy for my mama," Lida said. "But not today. I
return with husband." Then she looked at her own watch, for
longer than was necessary to tell the time. What was she
thinking? She looked quickly at Mac and then back to Karlis.
Was this a signal they had worked out? I will look at my watch,
then I will look at you, then the two of us— Whose husband
would she return with? And wasn't her mother—didn't she
say her mother—

"I give good price," Karlis said.

"Not today."

He maneuvered to take something out of his side pocket and handed her a small shiny box from which she extracted a painted lead soldier no taller than her pinkie, mounted on a square of metal so it could stand freely. "Field Marshal Suvorov," Karlis said. "You like? I have collection from all wars."

"Maybe for husband."

"I show you good project. Come." Karlis led her back around the curtain and into the front room. Eric followed. Mac turned to join the line, but I grabbed his arm as the others left. "I thought her mother was dead."

"What?"

"Her mother isn't dead?"

"Not that I know of."

"But last night at her hotel, didn't she say—" Mac shook his head. "At the bar, didn't she tell you—" He shook it again. "When she was crying, I thought she was telling you that her mother—" But I stopped in midsentence, as Mac's eyes dropped, veered to the pagoda birdcage at our feet while I felt my own flare open in fear. I had no idea what I had to fear, except what I saw on his face. Guilt. I knew now I had not witnessed its likeness all day, the deerlike fright in his eyes as he raised them to me. I was certain he was about to take flight.

"That's not what she was saying," he whispered. That was guilt and this would be confession. "I—" he said, and stopped and sighed. "Lida—" So this was where it would end. In a stranger's slum, on a street of naked women in storefront windows against their will, in a country I had hardly meant to visit. It would be over in fifteen seconds, at the end of his next sentence "It's complicated," he said softly. "I'll explain later."

I answered in a violent whisper: "What is going on here?"

He held his forefinger to his lips, hushing me.

"Mac, they don't even speak English!"

"Sparks, I told you, it's complicated, I'll—"

"Wasn't she talking about her mother?"

"Yes, but—"

"She kept saying, 'Mama.' "

"She was talking about—about us."

"Mac," Lida called out from the other side of the drapery. "Mac." She wanted to show him something, a trinket, a tin soldier, another little piece of her heart. So this was what Belhaloumi Jebel had heard last night, this was the crucial piece of evidence.

"What about you?" I said. If it was over, I was ready, very nearly ready, to let it end swiftly, unambiguously, like lightning.

But he said nothing, he just looked at me with droopy eyes like a dog who knows he is going to be scolded. He tried to draw his arms around me. "I'll explain all of it later, but right now—"

I lurched back and grabbed the front of his jacket, the place where lapels would have been. "Why was she crying?"

There was a clattering and then a whooshing noise, like someone flinging open a cloth shower curtain, the curtain rings banging against the rod, the sound of a flag snapping in a brisk wind. Still clutching Mac's jacket, I peered over his shoulder. Eric had flung back the velvet drapery and stuck his head in, one hand gripping the camera that sat on his shoulder. " 'Scuse me, we need some light in here." He turned to face Lida, and I could hear the camera click on and start to roll. Lida looked into the lens and smiled deeply. Then her eyes swerved forty-five degrees and met mine over Mac's shoulder, behind his back, and I could see her smile dim as she realized she was eye-to-eye with me and that was not what she'd had in mind. I was still waiting for an explosion, waiting for the end of the world, but she just summoned her smile again, raised a hand to her lips, blew a wistful kiss in our direction, and turned back to Eric. Then I saw her slip out the door. The entire exchange hadn't lasted more than five seconds.

"What's going on?" Mac said.

"I don't know."

He spun around and marched into the front room. "Where's Lida?"

"She's history," Eric said.

"What happened? What did she say?"

" 'Proschai,' " Karlis reported as cigarette smoke wafted from the stoking furnace of his mouth.

"Shit," Mac muttered, and ran from the flat.

I heard him charge the hallway and barrel down the stairs, the bouncing weight of his feet against the linoleum fading like the sound of a distant train. I looked to Eric for an explanation. "She wanted me to take her picture. I said there wasn't enough light. She said it didn't matter. Then she split."

"What does *proschai* mean?" I asked Karlis.

"Bye-bye."

Eric shrugged. "Could be worse," he said. "Could've meant Next year in Jerusalem."

He had a point, and maybe it was his reassuring logic and the steady, caring hand on my arm that kept me from running after Mac right away. If it was going to be goodbye, why not let them say it in private? I should have let them say hello in private, and I might have, had she not parachuted into my life in such obvious need. "Let's go," I said to Eric. Four or five minutes was plenty of time. It was all the time I had. "We have a plane to catch."

I turned to look at Karlis, who hadn't removed his coat or

hat or cigarette. He was still displaced, still suffering from a forty-five-year-old wound. Still hadn't found anyone to talk to except the dog, who had lain down under the loft bed on a flannel blanket chewed up along the edges, resting his chin against his extended forepaws, his gray coat and black face markings as striking as a Kabuki mask. You could do worse than confide in that dog.

"*Proschai* to you, Karlis," I heard Eric say. He held out his hand to shake, an apologetic gesture of bonhomie. "Merry Christmas and all the rest."

We must have been as much of a curiosity to Karlis as he had been to us. "Thanks," I mumbled, "for everything."

He nodded blankly and watched us leave. He knew I had nothing to thank him for, except having provided an exotic diversion for our afternoon. Walking down the stairs with Eric, I was already beginning to feel that the very worst was over, that our lives might really return, in Lida's word, to normal. But as I reached to open the downstairs door, I remembered her crying last night and Mac's refusal to tell me why. I ran through my meager Russian vocabulary and grew suspicious all over again. "*Dosvedanya* means goodbye," I told Eric. "*Proschai* has to mean something else."

"Kate, a little knowledge can be a dangerous thing."

It was nearly nightfall, but the lights Eric had promised hadn't come on yet, and I squinted to make out shapes, to find forms of life, up and down the sidewalk. Across the street and down a few doors were two shadowy figures facing each other, shrouded in a cloud of darkness between two storefront murals. I couldn't tell if they were talking or kissing, all I saw was that they were not moving. Neither was I.

"Come on," Eric said. I felt his hand on my shoulder, giving me a gentle push in their direction. "Don't forget that we won

the Cold War fair and square. We're almost outa here, kiddo,
we're almost home."

"But what if—"

"She's leaving. See that beige foreign body heading south?
That's her."

She had indeed turned around, alone, and begun walking
back the way we had come. But I still hadn't caught my breath.
I was halfway across the street before Mac noticed me. We
met at the curb and I saw him shake his head and smile, a
broad, unfocused smile, not at me but at something larger and
more mystifying, as if he'd just been told about the eighth
wonder of the world and couldn't believe it. Then he began
to laugh and laugh, a cackle that grew louder and more raucous
and frightening, a crazed, cruel-sounding laughter, utterly self-
involved. He was standing four feet from me, but it felt as if
there were miles between us. He clapped his hands once and
threw his head back triumphantly, and then shook it in a
rhythm of delighted wonder. Had I won, had I lost? Would
he tell me now or would I have to wait?

He smiled at me, a smile that at any other moment I would
have welcomed and trusted. "She just told me—you're going
to love this, Sparks—she just told me she was reporting to the
KGB the whole time. They contacted her after the first night
we spent together and said that if she wanted to keep seeing
me, it could be arranged, as long as—"

"That's all she was telling you just now?"

"That's all? That's all the State Department cared about.
Remember the friend from the KGB she called from my place
that night? She just said she'd never had any friends in the
Komitet. She wanted to keep seeing me, so she did whatever
they told her to."

"Then why was she crying?"

"When?"

"Last night."

He glanced toward her, to see that she was still moving, growing dimmer and smaller in the dusky light, and he glanced behind me and saw Eric skitter away from us, back up the street toward our hotel, and then I heard him sigh, not as if he was angry but as if he knew this was the moment of truth and he needed an extra dose of oxygen to get through it. I kept waiting for him to begin, and when he stuck a hand into the pocket of his coat, I thought it was because he was cold. He pulled something out of it that looked like a candy bar and offered it to me. A slab of Belgian chocolate? A consolation prize? "She didn't like the camera but she forgot about this once I turned it on." It was one of the cassette tapes I had pushed on him that morning. "I think we only used one side. It's mostly Russian, so when you want to listen, I'll translate. It's here, what you want to know." I took it and felt him draw his arm around me, lean his cold cheek against mine and hold it there. "Let's get going, Sparks. I'm sorry things ended up like this. I never imagined they would spin out the way they did. Come on, we've got our plane to catch."

Now that she was gone, had Mac become himself again, loving, open, eager to show me everything in his box of mementos? But I didn't move, I couldn't, except to pull away from him. Streetlights were coming on, doors to bars and peepshow palaces were flung open, and hawkers took positions beneath the canopies. Mac and I were the only other people in sight. "Is it so terrible you can't even say the words to me? You've already described every fuck the two of you had. Were there more you didn't mention? A multiple orgasm that slipped your mind? Any details you happened to—"

"It's on the tape, but if you have to know now, I'll tell you.

A week after I left Leningrad—" he turned away from me, and I think I knew then how the sentence would end, "she found out she was pregnant. Come on, let's get out of here. This place gives me the creeps." He held out his hand for me to take but I still couldn't move, or maybe all the movement was going on inside me, like the elevator in our hotel, shuddering and clanging up and down the shaft.

"But that doesn't mean—"

"She had an abortion."

That was when the pieces began to fall together. "So that's what he heard," I muttered.

"Who?"

"The guy at the bar." Her mother hadn't died, her baby had. Mac's baby.

"What guy?" Mac said.

"Why didn't she tell you back then?"

"Turns out she didn't tell me a lot of things."

"Would you have wanted the baby?"

"I didn't even know she—"

"Or is it her you want?"

"No, Sparks, I told you—"

"You haven't said anything since we got here, except 'poor Lida,' 'poor fucking Lida.' Is that what you said to her about me? 'Poor Kate, poor fucking Kate.' Kate, who doesn't have the nerve to have a kid because she's convinced everyone she cares about will die on her? Poor fucking Kate, who runs disaster central out of her office. Poor fucking Kate. Did you tell her how the people in my films can't wait to spill their whole life stories to me, to tell me some stupid joke they heard last week, because there's no one in their families left to talk to? Or is it poor Mac? Did you mention there's no fireworks when you get into bed with me, it's just, it's just—" That was when my voice gave out and the rest of me started to shake, and Mac just stood there astonished, waiting for the end of this sentence I had not known was in me. But when he saw I really couldn't speak, he took my hands in both of his and said my name and tried to put his arms around me.

"It's just a slow, deep river," I said quietly, holding back tears, pushing away from him, "and that's not what you want when you can have her, is it?"

"I can't have her, and I don't want her. I want you."

"What other secrets do you have?"

"I love you, Kate. *You.*"

"What else did she say in Russian that you didn't want me to know?"

"Are you listening? Do you hear me? I'm not here because I'm a nice guy or because I'm a guilt-ridden fucking Catholic who always tries to do the right thing. I'm here because of you."

He was right. I wasn't listening, though it wasn't thoughts of Lida pressing down on me, it was images of the girl I was sure it would have been, the sixteen-year-old who might have arrived last night at our hotel, this child at my door who looks just like mama, with a claim on Mac for the rest of his life, and I know it was not my finest moment, it was not my noblest thought, but all that went through my head was thank God she got rid of it, thank God she showed up here alone. "She told you she had an abortion and then what?"

"Sparks, we're going to miss our plane. There's a cab. Come on. I'll tell whatever you want to know."

It had begun to snow again, the flakes came down around us, hit the windshield of the taxi, and turned to water. The lights of the city seemed to run alongside the car, trying to keep up with us and falling behind at every corner. For a long time we were quiet, we looked out the windows, away from one another, as if we were still hearing the echo of what I had blurted out on the street about the fireworks and the slow, deep river. How much did he miss all that abandon, the furtive Cold War passion laced with vodka and Georgian wine, and the thrill of the whole world watching? How could I ever compete with that? I felt him reach across the seat for my hand and wrap his fingers around mine. There was all this love and corny affection between us, or there was before we got here, but my eyes were not capable of drawing him across a room, setting off the fire he had felt for her. I heard his voice, and I was sure the hard truth was coming. "When she called our house the other day, whenever it was, I had a fleeting fantasy she was going to tell me she had my child. It would have been—a replacement for Sam. It would have made me very happy. I kept picturing a boy like Sam. The only kid she talked about was her daughter, so I put my fantasy to rest, but when she showed up here early—I fell back on it. I got it into my head that her grand entrance was part of the surprise. 'Here's your boy. Isn't he fine?' I wasn't dwelling on it, I wasn't obsessing, they were just flashes, images that went through my head. When I saw she was alone, I let go of it, like a balloon. But when she told me about the baby, about the abortion, I went into a kind of tailspin, but inside. I was afraid to tell you, I couldn't—I knew you were upset, but I—I was sure if I said anything, you'd fly into a rage, you wouldn't let me see her today, and I had to. I couldn't just let her—I owed her something for what she went through."

"You owed me something too."

"You don't seem to understand that you won. *I* never thought of it as a competition, but since you did, you might as well accept your victory. I don't know why you can't."

"That's the first reasonable thing you've said since we got here. Maybe that's why."

"But I just told you—"

He stopped when he saw me shaking my head.

"What is it?" he said.

I felt dizzy at not knowing anymore what made sense, who was right, who was wrong, what I had won and what I had lost. I dropped my face into my raised hands and held it there as if it was injured, as if I might never be able to lift it again.

"Sparks, I never had any intention of betraying you, and there was nothing she could have done to make me. Believe me, she tried." He was quiet for a time, maybe thinking about how hard Lida had tried, or the way he had found me outside the door to Eric's room. I heard him swallow and felt his cold fingers around mine. "It must have seemed awfully threatening to you—but it never was. I tried to tell you, but you were so angry. You know I hate to fight—I just—I couldn't believe you'd think I'd lie to you. Have I ever given you any reason to think I would?" When I looked up to tell him I didn't know the answer to that either, he leaned forward and told the driver to let us off.

We had come to the edge of the glistening square we had first seen last night, our first stop on our way to the heart of all this darkness. I noticed the beautiful neon signs, shop windows lit up for Christmas with strings of blinking lights, the faint smell of chocolate, streetlights glowing a soft, golden yellow, and when I turned my head just slightly to the left, I saw Mac looking at me, squinting his eyes in sympathy. Was it that my eyes could not draw him across a room or that when he looked at me across our own rooms, so often I looked away, hauled out the cameras, the tape decks, Steenbecks, all the partitions I needed between me and the hazards of real life? He took my hand and we walked the half block to our hotel in silence, neither one of us ready to broach the only subject still left untouched.

Three weeks later, we have still not said a word about it. When we get into bed at night, he holds me as if I am made of glass, as if I am in mourning. Does he want permission? Is he waiting for me to make the first move, or does he just imagine we will get back to the seashore somehow or other, if not tonight, maybe tomorrow? Does he remember our fireworks in the cabin, the way they came after all those weeks of tears and timidity? I think I believe that he loves me, but what else hasn't he said, what else does he keep to himself?

SEVENTEEN

▼

All through Turkey, I kept the cassette tape he had given back to me buried at the bottom of my suitcase like contraband, and when we came home, five days early, I gave everything to Eric and asked him to deal with the lab.

What will happen if I listen to it now?

What will happen if I don't?

I will miss the particular timbre of their intimacy, the sultry swagger of her voice, the silences in which Mac groped for words like a man who has misplaced the structure of his own language. I will miss being reminded of the way Lida took Mac's hand across the table and did what she did with it, there in the middle of the Café d'Or. I made Mac tell me the highlights on the plane on our way to Istanbul, and whenever he would come to a standstill and sort of shrug, like that was about it, he couldn't remember another thing, I'd tell him to go on, to keep trying, and there was always something more.

I dread what I am about to hear, but I'd forgotten there was more picture to see. On the screen are close-ups of Lida's exit from Karlis's flat. She smiles, she turns to look for Mac, she mouths the word *proschai*. But Eric was right: there really wasn't enough light. The picture is spectral and dark, as if shot inside a coal mine with only a lantern. There's a sliver of light glinting off Lida's two front teeth.

I am thinking of her histrionic entrances and exits, of the way she can hold a crowd, plunge into the center of my life and erupt like a natural disaster. She is all impulse, hunger, and audacity. She is three thousand miles away, and it is not far enough.

I crawl the picture forward, expecting her voice and Mac's voice, expecting to see whatever filler footage the lab laid down next to the sound track to match the length of it, a clip of an old train wreck, a government training film, or a faded print of a Preston Sturges movie, the usual stuff discarded by studios and networks that you find on film-lab shelves, good for nothing except to fill the spaces between the sprockets.

But what comes up on the screen astounds me. It looks like Brussels: slick, sweeping pans of the Palais de Justice, the Palais Royal, a sprawling, verdant park, a wide shot of the Grand'-Place, but the entire city is drenched in sunlight. I must be looking at stock footage produced for the Belgian Tourist Bureau on one of the three sunny days of the year. Who else would care to leave such a misleading impression of the weather? And who but Eric would have thought to track it down and instruct the lab to splice it in right here? It's another sly message for me, a belated Christmas present, an ingenious reminder of the Magritte painting he thinks ought to exist: the man gripping the handle of an open umbrella with a stunning blue sky up above.

I have almost forgotten I am about to hear Lida and Mac wrestle over love.

But that's not her voice: it's another woman, a thin, mealy monotone, speaking what must be her words in English: "It was very good back then, your Russian." I hear Lida's voice, in Russian, on the other sound track, much softer.

"I haven't spoken a word since Leningrad," Mac says. "It's like learning to walk again. I keep tripping and falling down." I hear his halting Russian, very softly, and a dull man speaking his words in broadcaster's English on the other sound track, louder than the Russian. "You know, I never told you where I learned it."

There are faint background noises, the sounds of spoons clacking against coffee cups, against a table, a wooden chair being pushed along a tile floor, but on the screen are still sunny street scenes of Brussels, the elegant windows of Neuhaus and Leonidas and Godiva, the pinched, winding alleys of the Ilot Sacré, restaurants cheek by jowl and a thousand suntanned tourists.

"University, no? That's what you told me."

"I lied. I learned in the army, in the fifties. I spent a year in California studying and two years sitting in a van at the edge of West Germany with headphones on, listening in on Soviet military phone calls, translating—they're called communications intercepts. We picked up backscatter from military commands. I bet you didn't know we had a dictionary— the Russians had one just like it—that listed Russian words by syllables, so that if we could only pick up the last syllable of a word, we could look that up and see all the words that ended with that syllable."

. "I love it! You listened to my father give orders!"

"Or talk to your mother about your days in kindergarten."

"You told me other lies, my darling, or was that the only one?"

"I lied about my job in Leningrad."

"You weren't the consul? You didn't give out visas?"

He must have been shaking his head.

"What did you do there all those months?"

"Nothing."

"That's a good job, nothing. You need special training?"

"I filled up the days. I listened to the radio to practice my Russian. I helped out a few American tourists in a jam. Issued three or four visas."

"So you were a spy, just like they thought."

"More like a mannequin. Do you want more coffee? *Encore deux cafés, s'il vous plaît.* In New York one night back then, near the United Nations, a group of FBI agents beat up a KGB agent. The KGB retaliated by beating up a CIA agent in Leningrad. Beat him up exactly the same way, broke his glasses, broke his nose. This was standard, this kind of identical retaliation, up until the very end. We expelled the KGB agent, so of course the Russians expelled the CIA agent from Leningrad. While the CIA trained a replacement, they wanted to send someone over to confuse the KGB, so when the actual spy showed up, the theory went, he could slip in more or less undetected. The CIA asked to borrow a body from the State Department to help muddy the waters. My name came up on the computer: Russian-speaking Foreign Service officers. I was the only one available. You sure you don't want another croissant, a piece of pastry? Most of the people at the consulate didn't know why I was there. My wife was the only one I could tell the truth to."

There is a long, scratchy silence, the ambient noise of the

café. Perhaps Lida is thinking: The KGB would have loved to know this, but me, I never cared a hang what you did for a living. "Remember the day you taught me to drive?"

"*Tried* to teach you to drive."

"And I almost killed us both." She bursts into laughter, laughing almost as hard as she had that day on the road to Pavlovsk.

"As we shot down that hill, I was sure we were going to die. When we didn't, I was sure we'd never get out of the mud, and I'd owe the consulate a car. And I'd be deported on the next plane."

"The problem was"—she is still laughing—"I wasn't sure how to change gears."

"Or steer."

"Now I talk on my car phone and change gears at the same time! But steering is still a bit of a problem. When I first came to France, I took driving lessons. You should have seen! My poor husband, I thought he would divorce me. The driving teacher, one day he leaned over and said, 'You are a bright woman with good coordination, so why is it so difficult for you to—' "

"Lida, there's something—"

"It was because whenever I looked into the mirror on the right side of the car, I would look for too long and drift into the next lane. What a mess!"

"Lida, why didn't you tell me you were pregnant?"

She sighs and the translator sighs too, and I hear what sounds like a spoon tapping the edge of a saucer. "I explained last night, Mama told me not to." Her voice has dropped, so low I imagine Mac having to lean across the table just to hear her. "She told me to have the abortion and forget you."

"But if you were pregnant with my child—"

"I was very young and foolish, and last night, I was so full of emotion at seeing you." Her voice sounds entirely different, calm and focused. She is finally present. It has been her romance with Mac, not her driving lessons, that she has wanted to talk about.

"So you would have kept the baby if your mother hadn't—"

"We were very good together, weren't we, Mac?"

"You could have written to me about it. The KGB wouldn't have cared. They couldn't have used it against you."

"You remember the way we made love together?"

"Of course."

"And the time we made love in your kitchen? I sat on the countertop and you—"

"I—yes. Of course."

"The bottle of Joy you bought me when you left—now that I am a rich capitalist, I wear it all the time."

"I didn't know that."

"You don't smell it?"

She leans across the table, presenting the nape of her neck, waiting for a kiss.

"I'm not . . . my nose isn't . . . it's very nice."

"I was just thinking, we could go back to St. Petersburg. Would you like that, my love?" He must be sitting there so still and mute that she takes his silence as consent, and maybe he is kicking the idea around, or marshaling his courage to turn her down. "We'll get a room at the Astoria with a view of the Neva and make love until dawn, the way we used to."

I am listening for him to say no, to make her stop talking like this, to set her straight the way he told me he had. But it's as if he's forgotten his lines. Is this the place where she grabs his hand and thrusts it to her breast? Is this a place where he might have looked into her eyes and remembered the way they could draw him across a room and into arms that made him swell in seconds? Is this a place he might have wondered when and where and Jesus Christ, why the hell not? Were there moments he wavered, or were these silences his refuge from the anguish of turning her down, this man who can't bear to disappoint the people he cares about, who sometimes goes so far out of his way not to hurt one person's feelings that he ends up wounding everyone? "Lida, if I weren't married, it would be—"

"Mama told me to forget about you, she said you were no good, you were never coming back. But how could I? How do I stop feeling love? I am Russian. In the West, you are polite, you laugh, you visit your friends, but it's all *here*, not *here*." She points to her head and then her heart. "In Paris, people say to me, 'Lida, you are so emotional all the time.' I'm a little bit of a freak, you know, but *this*"—pointing again to her heart—"is where I live. My husband lives *here*, with the rest of the French. He doesn't understand me, not the way you do, Mac."

"Lida, I'm very moved you feel so much for me, but you met my wife last night. She trusts me, she wouldn't—"

"You were everything to me. I waited years for you to send for me. And now you're here."

"I—I'm very happy to see you too."

"Show me, my darling."

There is a long silence on the sound track, the movement of cups and saucers, the hiss of an espresso maker spewing hot milk into a cup of cappuccino. On the screen are more monuments of Brussels, cathedrals, universities, the modern subway system, the stations decorated with paintings, sculpture, colorful wall tiles. The genteel wonders of Brussels, a city of

diplomats, of industry, commerce, of sober international ne-
gotiation, a city that stood up to the Nazis for days you could
count on the fingers of one hand. Lida could teach them a
thing or two about resolve, about hanging on to what's yours
for dear life.

"Now we can have our child. I will give you another son,
since you miss your boy so much."

"Lida, I can't." The man translating his words into English
says them loud and clear, though I hear Mac stumble in
Russian on the other sound track. But is what I hear his fragile
Russian or his fragile conviction? "My wife and I are—"

"Don't tell her, the way you told your other wife. There's
no reason to hurt anyone. We don't need to have the child.
You can stay with your wife and we'll meet in Europe or New
York. This spring I go to Atlanta for business. Is that near
you?"

"I would make my wife very unhappy if I—"

"Let me love you after all this time."

"But, Lida—"

"Just tell me yes."

There were to be no more surprises, but every frame, every
syllable, every second of Mac's silence, is a blow. I know I
took off my clothes for another man and let him touch me in
places that are private, but Mac was spared the sight of it, and
he has not asked for details. The way I have. I'm the one who
wants to wallow in all this, pick it apart, get to the bottom,
like a crazed deep-sea diver searching for sunken treasure where
only debris has been sighted.

"Lida, no one could have sent for you in those days. The
President couldn't have sent for you." He wants to change the
subject from her passion to his responsibility. He wants to
unburden himself of some of the guilt he has carried all these

years for the way he left, waving goodbye on a street corner in the dark, and having to leave her *there*, an easy target for KGB practice. He had no idea that she was reporting to them two and three times a week. That she told them everything she could remember about the consul general's cocktail party, the consul general, his house, and his nanny, Susan Pollet. She answered their ridiculous questions only so they would let her return every night to his bed.

"But I was sure," she tells him in Brussels, "that an American man working for the government, in an important position—"

"A consul is not important. A man pretending to be a consul is even less important."

"All of a sudden you stopped writing. It was like we were on a boat and you fell overboard."

"Didn't Susan tell you about the investigation?" He is genuinely surprised. Had she never understood what had happened three months after he returned?

"Yes, but when the difficult part was over, I thought you would write again and let me know—"

"In my last letter, I said it would be the last letter. I told you to forget about me."

"But I thought that when you were out of danger, maybe in a year or two—"

"It was very serious, Lida. They almost fired me. They showed your photographs to the Marine guards in Leningrad and Moscow, to see if you looked familiar, if you were an agent or a prostitute. When they found out you weren't—the principal reason I wasn't fired was that there was no evidence linking you to the KGB. They told me I could write one last letter. But I didn't explain any of this, because I knew they were reading our mail. I didn't want you to get into more trouble with the KGB."

"After you left, they wanted me to be a prostitute for them. To follow around this foreigner and that foreigner, to go to bed with all of them. I told them no. I said absolutely not. I was with you because I loved you, but that didn't mean I would—that's why I lost my two jobs, because I wouldn't cooperate. But your last letter was so remote, I was sure you had stopped loving me. It was worse than losing twenty jobs."

"If there had been some way for us to—"

"Now there is, Mac. Even in Russia there is no more Komitet. No one to listen to our lovemaking. This summer during our revolution, and when the Berlin Wall came down, I couldn't turn off the TV. I'd stay up all night watching the news and crying. I kept saying to myself, 'What if this had happened seventeen years ago?' I could have left and married you. I knew I had to find my one great love after all this time, and now that I've found you—"

"I'm in a different marriage than when you knew me, Lida. We're very happy together. My wife trusts me. I couldn't do this to her."

"Stop talking about her! Do *you* want me?"

"Lida, she's not going to disappear, and I don't want her to. I'm not going to do anything to push her away."

"I met her, Mac, she is not the right woman for you, she is not—"

"She is, Lida."

"What does she have that I don't? How could she—"

"She has me. She trusts me."

"But your other wife—"

"She was different. It was a different time in my life."

There are many seconds of silence, and the clatter of spoons and dishes and what sounds like a child speaking French nearby. "I just remembered something I couldn't tell you in Leningrad," Mac says softly.

"What is it?" she answers quickly, hungrily.

"It's not a big deal, really, it's not, but it just came to me. It's about Baryshnikov. I knew the night I left that he had defected the night before. We'd gotten a cable that afternoon. I didn't tell you because I was sure it would upset you, with everyone leaving but you."

I hear nothing for ten or fifteen seconds, and then, very softly, "I'm sorry to cry again. I was just thinking about that night we saw him. He was very beautiful, wasn't he? *The Creation of the World*. Curled up on the stage as tight as a snake." Then she begins to laugh, but it comes from the top of her throat, a long way from her famous heart. "My friends in Leningrad used to say the only reason he defected was because he wanted more money, because he was getting too big for his britches. Did they say that in America?"

Mac is taken aback by her tears, her bright effort to change the subject, and by what sounds like a touch of anger she is trying to keep under wraps. "Lida, I'm so sorry. Leningrad was wonderful. What we had there—I'll never forget. You were so special to me. You know how much I cared for you. I told you our last night together. Don't you remember? For years—" He started to say he used to keep her photograph out but changed his mind. He didn't want to suggest that his own desire had been so concrete, that for years between involvements, between real women, he used to take the picture out and prop it on the bookcase. There on the shelf, a decade later, she was like a soldier's pinup, a wonderful idea to look

forward to, look back on, a momentary escape from every kind
of loneliness, and a shot in the arm. I am worthy because she
once loved me to distraction. But he never imagined that she
might still. "For years, I thought about you. I was thrilled
when you called. I thought about you during the coup. I looked
for you on TV, in all the pictures from Leningrad. I knew if
you were there, you'd be leading the crowds. I was so happy
to hear you were out, married, with your child—I'm sorry we
can't—"

"You think he's heroic, Baryshnikov, because he defected?
Because he pranced away from his bus with his ballet slippers
and tutu? You're right, it's no big deal. Russians like me—
we went through hell to get out." Perhaps the tears had been
her last resort, and when they failed to move Mac to the place
she had wanted him, her pain turned full force into anger. "I
was six months pregnant before they let me go. I hadn't seen
Philippe since our wedding. We were married for three days,
then nothing for six months, on account of those bastards. We
made the baby right away, because we knew that if I was
pregnant they would have to give me a visa, because the Helsinki Accords said that husband and wife had to be together
if there was going to be a baby.

"Philippe had to go home to Paris after the wedding, because
he had spent all his money visiting me, flying his family to
the wedding. In those days, it cost a fortune to travel without
a tour, and there were Mama and me, in our lousy apartment
as big as this table." I am surprised by her bitterness, and even
more surprised that it fades so quickly. "I remember that first
night with you, I went snooping around every room in your
place. It was like the Hermitage!"

"You ran around in a frenzy."

"I remember thinking that you were *so* old. I was just going to have a drink with you and leave, because I was taught to be kind to old people! So much for charity!"

She has made herself laugh again, and Mac too, but the sound is a strange counterpoint to the black-and-white filler coming up on the screen. It looks like a thirties gangster movie, but it's been spliced in upside down, which means that the action is taking place in reverse. I close my eyes against the strain of looking at it.

"When did you finally get out?"

"October first, 1983. I remember the date like it's my birthday. I was out to here with Sonya, as big as a watermelon. Every week for six months, I'd go up and down Nevsky like a street sweeper, to the ministry of this and that. 'Look at me! I must have my visa! You must abide by the treaty!' 'Lady, don't bother us with your stinking problems.' 'So this is how you uphold the Helsinki Accords?' 'Shut up or you will never see your husband.' Really, they said these things to me. What for? You know, Mac, it's such a shame that you couldn't tell me in your last letter what had happened with the investigation, because all these years I had no idea you really cared for me. I thought you were tired of me and—"

"Lida, it would have been impossible for us. I was still married, and they might never have let you out. Look at what you went through years later."

She is silent for a moment. She has tried the front door, the back door, the windows, every last entrance to his heart. "I suppose you're right."

"Why did they let you leave?"

"Three months passed, four months, *five* months, almost six to the day. I called Philippe and said, 'You must contact the Red Cross and tell them what's going on, tell them to apply more pressure.' Would you believe, two days later, I got a call to pick up the visa? But that wasn't the end of my troubles. At the airport—here I am with all my baggage, my entire life in these bags—they took every single bag apart, like animals. They turned everything inside out and left it on the ground. Then they said, 'Go! Get out of here!' 'But I can't. I need help. Can't you see, I'm pregnant. My things are all over.' 'Go in there now.' 'Where?' 'The next room.' Well, in the next room, a little room with no windows, there is a witch who says to me, 'Strip.' 'What?' 'You heard me, take off everything.' 'What is this? What are you talking about?' 'You know what I m talking about. You heard me, bitch. Strip!' 'But why?' 'I told you to shut your mouth.'

  "I said to this woman, 'Keep your hands off me.' She came up to my nose. 'We know you are smuggling out diamonds.' Can you believe it? I looked her in the eye and said, 'The only thing I've got up there is a picture of Lenin.' She backed off and let me go. But outside this room, my clothes were everywhere. I started to pick them up, with my belly out to here, and some American tourists saw me, a big tour group. They came right over, packed, and helped me carry all the bags to the gate We were on the same flight to Paris, and when I went into the plane and took my seat, they took such good care of me. 'Oh, you are pregnant, you must rest.' I said to them, 'I love my country so much. Why do people do these things? I love my country more than that awful woman. She's only jealous of me because I'm leaving.' The Americans said, 'Lida, it's time to forget. You're going to see your husband and start a new life.' One man, such a kind man, sat with me the whole flight, and we talked. You can't imagine how nervous I was. I had never been out of Russia. The best moment—the moment I'll always remember—was when we landed in Paris. We were on the ground at the gate, but no one moved in the whole plane, except me. I stood up, expecting everyone would too. But nothing. I looked and looked at all the faces sitting there, and suddenly this entire planeload of people burst into applause. For me. They said"—this she said to Mac in English—" 'Welcome to West, Lida. You are home now.' I cried. Are those tears I see in your eyes? You know, I think inside you are really Russian. So much passion. Remember the day we went to Piskarev and you cried? That was when you told me you were leaving. You remember my Jewish husband who was going to Israel? He went first to Israel, then Oregon. He works for Nike. I told him, in a few years, let's make a deal and bring running shoes to Russia. *After* the dirty phone calls." She laughs and Mac laughs, and for a few seconds neither of them says anything. "I can't believe you're sitting here across from me. For years I had no other relations, because you were so real, because I was sure I would see you again. Of course, I kept your letters, but you know, I have no picture. We have a superstition in Russia—"

"I remember. If you exchange pictures—"

"Do you have a camera with you?"

"At the hotel."

"I want to take a picture of you today. Let's go there to pick up your camera."

"Did Susan know you were pregnant?"

"Of course. She came to Paris when Sonya was born. She is like Sonya's aunt."

"I don't mean with Sonya."

"I told her not to tell you."

"But why?"

"Don't be angry with me, Mac."

"I had a right to know. And I would have wanted to comfort you."

"But Mama told me that—"

"Forget your mother for a minute, Lida, just tell me—"

Then the sound tracks end and the picture goes white. I'm startled to see the rolls run out and the take-up plates spin with no resistance, startled that this is where it ends, up in the air, in midsentence. But what was I expecting? A happy ending? I lean back into the arms of the padded gray swivel chair in which I have sat upright, as if on a piano bench, for almost two hours, and take a deep breath. I roll the chair away from the Steenbeck and stand to stretch my arms, my torso, and look at my watch. Four more hours till midnight, till my self-inflicted deadline. I am still circling the site of the buried treasure, a long way from laying my hands on it.

The only light in this windowless room is the sixty-watt gooseneck lamp on the typing table by my elbow, the table on which I've stacked all the footage. The place looks like a cave, an eerie basement piled high with strange-looking machines, metal shelves holding hundreds of boxes of film, trash cans filled with discarded ribbons of celluloid. I light the last cigarette in the pack, pull hard on it, and watch the smoke drift out of my mouth with a peculiar interest, as if this is some new talent I've acquired and I'm astonished at what I can do.

Then I notice the snapshot of Lida I snitched from Mac's mementoes yesterday and pluck it from its perch at the base of the Steenbeck screen. I carry it across the room and prop it on a shelf at eye level. Move it down two shelves, lean it against a row of boxes each labeled ABIDJAN 1990, and study her smile, her nipples, the triangle of darkness at the place her thighs meet.

What does the protagonist want and what are the obstacles? She wants Mac and she can't have him. There's the State Department in her way, the KGB, Mac's first wife, and now his second. She hasn't got a prayer.

But I knew all this two hours ago.

I knew it three weeks ago.

What do I expect to see here? Who am I looking for?

I left Turkey five days early because she was everywhere, because I had to get away from everything that reminded me of her, and home seemed like a move in the right direction, but here we are again, on my turf now. Why does it feel as if she is still in charge, still calling the shots, like I have become a walk-on character in my own marriage? I wander across the room and crush out the cigarette in the ashtray on the typing table that's wedged between stacks of footage. Before I leave tonight I have to rewind all of it and stick it back in the boxes, or throw it away, or put it aside to use for filler. But if I were going to make something of it, where would I begin—with Lida in Leningrad or me in Brussels? With Lida in Mac's bed, or me in his bed, the night he told me the story of their affair? Is it her story or is it mine?

Which one of us is the protagonist after all?

I look back at the snapshot of Lida and roll my chair across the floor so I can see her up close. What keeps this drama going is my fascination with her, not hers with Mac. Or even Mac's with her. He had told me the story of their romance all right, but once I laid eyes on her myself, and saw how vivid it still was to her, I started believing her version. I took the whole thing up a few notches, added an extra measure of whipped cream to the recipe, another dollop of lust. I did what she had done; I remembered their story too well, and forgot completely about my own. The only time Mac thinks of her, he tells me now, is when I bring her up. If he can put her aside, if he can live without her, why can't I? I am staring at her nude photograph, kneeling on the damp, twisted sheets of Mac's bed in Leningrad, serving up her luscious breasts to him once more. I am sifting through the syllables of her speech, the highlights of her life, the palpitations of her famous heart, taking note of every loss she has endured from Russia to France, from Leningrad to St. Petersburg.

She is cradling her breasts for the benefit of the cameraman, but in Brussels I saw her cry like a child and fling herself at Mac with an audience watching, a movie camera rolling. Me, I wait until I am alone in the dark to shed a single tear. I weep when her plane lands in Paris and the Americans clap and say, "Welcome to West, Lida. You are home now." I weep when Eric whispers my name and tries to rescue me from my own pitiful seduction. At least Lida could say that she wanted the man she tried to bed, that she acted out of passion, not fear.

Can it be that I am obsessed with the palpitations of her famous heart because I want a piece of it? And I gape at this wrinkled black-and-white snapshot pilfered from Mac's box of mementos, at her naked body perched on his bed, because I want to love him with that kind of abandon, to throw off my shroud, the widow's weeds I cling to like the old women who visit Piskarev every week, like poor Karlis, who hasn't found anyone to talk to in forty-five years.

I stare at the photograph and imagine my mother in our living room in Oceanside Gardens, with her tubes of oil paint, her toothpicks and cotton balls, trying to follow the instructions for this one. Hair: auburn. Complexion: fair. Eyes: as bright

as Magritte's bluest sky. Intentions: the usual. Obstacles: extraordinary. Results: you can't say she didn't try. And I see
myself at five or six, peering down the hall at her, when she
is sure I am in the other room, sound asleep. What was I
doing there? Protecting her, waiting up for him, standing back
to study the lines and shadows of their faces? Were they ever
in the same room for long enough to look at each other without
arguing, my mother and father, or were they always trying to
look away, my mother with her photographs and her heartache, my father with his binoculars? I go all the way to Turkey
to study the streets of my grandfather's childhood and end up
here, tonight, stuck on the streets of my own, looking up into
the windows of the apartments where we lived as my father
looks out, looking everywhere but where we were. His hunger
to witness the whole world from far away as long as he did not
have to notice the rest of us at his feet. Is that what I'm doing
with Lida, locked in battle with a woman who was supposed
to stay in the Plexiglas frame in Mac's boxes of mementos,
beautiful and harmless, as well preserved as the body of Lenin?
Is it so much easier to look at her than myself? I am still
running from the dinner table of my childhood to the bedroom
closet, to sit out the storm in something like safety. Instead of
fighting for my place at the table, my position in the family,
I shoot film, stick microphones in people's faces, and make
them tell me where it hurts.

As if I don't already know.

The bulletproof glass partitions between me and the hazards
of real life. Between me and the pleasures of real life. This
body I live in like it's on loan to me, some old thing I've
borrowed and haven't really taken possession of. Been too busy,
had too many deadlines, too much money to raise to keep the

machinery running, the images moving at twenty-four frames a second.

I put the picture of Lida aside and move the typing table stacked with rolls of footage from my right elbow to my left, so I can begin to rewind each reel. It should take twenty minutes or half an hour to get everything wound in the right direction. A piece of her famous heart. Not a big piece. That wouldn't be my style. I'm thinking of a tiny piece, a piece the size of a diamond. When I'm finished rewinding the footage, I'll put the rolls back into the boxes I brought them in and carry them up Sixth Avenue to our apartment for the night, and tell Mac what I've just decided to do with them. It will please him, my decisiveness, and he might ask what it was I saw and heard tonight that led me to this place. Or he might just stand back and enjoy the scenery, the unaccustomed calm in my eyes, my voice, my kiss. I don't know if I'm ready to talk to him yet, and maybe that is not where I should set my sights. It will take getting used to—that this is not really about words. But with or without them, we will get around to taking Otis for his walk, the way we do every night, and then put in an appearance at Nan's annual New Year's Eve bash, have something to eat and a glass of champagne, see a few friends we haven't seen since before our trip to Turkey. They will want to know how the shoot went in Istanbul, and Mac will answer first.

"Wonderful," he'll tell them, diplomat that he is.

"Like a dream," I'll chime in. "We start editing next week."

But between now and then, I'm going to look through all this footage again. I'm going to come back here tomorrow—tomorrow afternoon—with a thermos of coffee and a notebook and start over. A piece not much bigger than a diamond.

Something I can hide just about anywhere and take out on special occasions, when I need to make a splashy entrance or exit, when I need to flaunt my assets, my net worth, my love. There might be notes for a documentary in all this, raw material for a feature, a story line I couldn't see until now. There might be something I can use here after all.

ACKNOWLEDGMENTS

I'd like to thank the District of Columbia Commission on the Arts and Humanities, the Virginia Center for the Creative Arts, and the Corporation of Yaddo for their generous support during the writing of this book.

It could not have been written without help from filmmakers Pamela Briggs, Virginia Quesada, Virginia Durrin, and most especially David Petersen, who taught me most of what Kate knows about making movies.

James Sanders offered wonderful insights into the history and architecture of Brussels.

Andrea Murphy at the Belgian Embassy in Washington was unfailingly generous and helpful.

Friends in St. Petersburg—Katya Mikhailova, Elena Zelinskaya, and Alexander Bransky—made it possible for me to imagine the city at a very different time from the present. Alexa Scanziani helped make the present a great adventure. I'm grateful to O.P.G., for stories about these days and those, and to friends here whose careful readings of the manuscript guided me to the end.